SUPER HERO PLAYBOOK

LESSONS IN LIFE FROM YOUR FAVORITE SUPERHEROES

BY RANDALL LOTOWYCZ

ART BY TIM PALIN

LESSONS

SUPER HERO PLAYBOOK

LESSONS IN LIFE FROM YOUR FAVORITE SUPERHEROES

*For Peter Wolff, the superhero
I like even more than Superman.*
– Randall Lotowycz

*For Brooke, Lily, and Luke...because
they totally rule! Pow! Zap! Boom!*
– Tim Palin

Library of Congress Cataloging-in-Publication Data available upon request.
ISBN: 9781947458765

Duopress books are available at special discounts when purchased in bulk for sales promotions as well as for fund-raising or educational use. Special editions can be created to specification. Contact us at hello@duopressbooks.com for more information.

Manufactured in China
10 9 8 7 6 5 4 3 2 1
Duopress LLC
8 Market Place, Suite 300, Baltimore, MD 21202, Distributed by Workman Publishing Company, Inc.
Published simultaneously in Canada by Thomas Allen & Son Limited.
To order: hello@duopressbooks.com
www.duopressbooks.com
www.workman.com
Book design: Jeff Shake
Art direction: Kelley Lanuto, Kalanuto Design

INTRODUCTION
SUPERHEROES ARE AWESOME

Superheroes are awesome. They have cool suits and fantastic powers. They fight bad guys and save the world over and over again. It is fun to pretend to be like them. You might tie a towel around your neck like a cape or poke holes in a wool hat and pull it over your face like a mask. But what if you wanted to do more than just pretend to be a superhero? What if you actually wanted to be one?

Every superhero has an amazing origin story that explains how they became who they are. But you can't go trying to recreate that. After all, you are not an alien like Superman, and if a radioactive spider bit you, you'd probably get sick instead of turning into Spider-Man. Just because you cannot repeat their origins, that does not mean you cannot be a superhero.

Behind every mask and superpower, you will find very real and very valuable qualities that these superheroes have. These traits are the things that make them put on their tights every morning and keep doing good. These traits can all be yours if you want them!

In your hands is a special journey into the stories of 20 of the greatest superheroes and teams. (If your favorite superhero is missing, let us know, and we'll see about adding them if we do another book.) We will dig a little deeper past these superheroes' origin stories to reveal what makes them so powerful. You will discover what makes their minds and hearts so strong. Every step along the way, you will also see how you can be just like them. And then you can show the world just how great of a superhero you are.

Are you up for the challenge?
I knew you would be. Let's get started!

SUPERMAN
THE BRIGHTEST IN THE SKY

The last son of a dying planet came to Earth with abilities greater than those of mortal humans...but more importantly, he always aspires to do what's right and inspires others to do the same.

Minutes before the planet Krypton exploded, Jor-El and Lara placed their baby, Kal-El, in a rocket ship and launched him into space. The rocket ship traveled across the universe, carrying Kal-El to Earth, where the kind farm couple Jonathan and Martha Kent found and adopted him. Given the name Clark by his new parents, the child learned he had many special abilities such as superhuman strength, amazing speed, and the ability to fly, which he decided to use to help others. When Clark grew up, he was known by another name: Superman. He was always friendly and eager to help. People looked up to Superman, and not just because he flew through the sky.

SUPERMAN

Jor-El told his son in a recorded message that the people of Earth "can be a great people, Kal-El. They wish to be. They only lack the light to show the way. For this reason above all, their capacity for good, I have sent them you, my only son." Jor-El believed his son, who would one day become Superman, could be a great **role model** to everyone on Earth.

A role model is someone who inspires people to be better and try harder. They set examples that others want to follow.

It would be awesome to lift mountains like they were small rocks or fly around the world in seconds, but you do not need to do those things to be like Superman. Just be a role model! You can be one by setting a good example for others, such as your friends, classmates, and siblings. You can even be a role model for adults. Just tell them Superman sent ya!

Stick with Your Values

Superman fought for truth and justice. Those were his values. To be a good role model, you have to follow a clear set of values or rules. The easy part is learning your values, like being honest, fair, kind, and respectful. The hard part is living by them every day. Does that sound like something only Superman could do? Don't worry! His powers developed over time as he grew up. It might take you a little time to become a good role model.

Ways to Be a Role Model

- Do not tell lies.
- Never cheat.
- Offer help to people who need it.
- Be nice to everyone.

Even Role Models Need Role Models

Superman had a couple of good role models of his own with his adopted Earth parents, the Kents. He learned most of his strong values from them as they raised him in Smallville, Kansas. Superman may have gotten his powers from his birth parents on Krypton, but the Kents showed him how to be a great person.

A Flyby Friend

Even when Superman was busy saving the day, he always took the time to help someone in need. When he saw someone who was sad, he said, "It's never as bad as it seems. You're much stronger than you think you are. Trust me." He was **encouraging** the sad person.

Encourage means you show support about something.

As a role model, always keep a lookout for people who might be having a bad day. Try to cheer them up. If a teammate is worried because the team has lost a few games, tell them not to give up and to think about how to win the next game. You can encourage your friends to be hopeful by staying hopeful yourself.

Symbol of Hope

That symbol on Superman's chest is not just the letter S for his name. It is the symbol for hope in Kryptonian, the language people spoke on Krypton. If you were going to make your own symbol of hope, what would it look like? Try drawing your own and share it with friends.

When people saw Superman flying through the air, they would say, "Look, up in the sky!" When you are a role model, people will look up to you even when your feet are firmly on the ground.

13

BLACK PANTHER

LEADERS ARE MADE, NOT BORN

The noble king of a secretive African nation selflessly protects his people...but, leadership is service, and Black Panther must be a king to all.

The Eastern African nation of Wakanda was full of secrets and surprises. It was one of the most advanced countries in the world, but you would never know it from the outside. Its futuristic cities and technology were all built with Vibranium, a special metal found only in Wakanda. For years, Wakanda's kings kept the nation's great secrets hidden from the rest of the world. Each king also protected Wakanda as a masked warrior known as the Black Panther. After King T'Chaka died, his son Prince T'Challa took over as the new Black Panther. He had to learn how to be a leader. He made the incredibly tough decision to introduce both Black Panther and Wakanda to the rest of the world.

If you want to be a leader like Black Panther, you need to have a good group of people supporting you. Black Panther had many smart people with him, like his mother Ramonda, his sister Shuri, and his friends Nakia and W'Kabi. If they did not agree with Black Panther, they told him. Instead of ignoring their **constructive criticism**, Black Panther listened to his friends to help make his decisions. If you are the captain of a sports team or lead a school club, make sure you listen to everyone's ideas and not do only what you want to do.

Black Panther became a great leader by listening to what others have to say and being open to constructive criticism.

Listening to Everyone Means EVERYONE

It is easy to listen to your friends and family members, but it is just as important to listen to people you might not like. When the villain Killmonger tried to take over Wakanda, he planned to do many bad things. Black Panther stopped Killmonger, but he also learned from the bad guy that the world needed Wakanda's technology. Killmonger definitely wasn't offering constructive criticism when he almost killed Black Panther, but he still helped the hero see how to do things better. Yes, even bad guys can have good ideas when they're not thinking about taking over the world!

If you get assigned a group project with someone you do not like, you still have to do the project. Even if the person is not nice to you, they could have some good ideas about the project. You should listen to them like you would listen to a friend.

ZAP!

Constructive criticism is a way to tell someone how they can change or do something better.

17

Never Settle for "Good Enough"

Black Panther's little sister Shuri was one of the smartest people in the world. He trusted her to be in charge of making all of Wakanda's technology because she was a great inventor. Black Panther liked the suit he wore in battle, but Shuri wanted to make him an even better one. Shuri taught him an important lesson when she said, "Just because something works does not mean it cannot be improved." Leaders should always try to make things better.

See, even younger siblings can teach you stuff!

OH!

Hard Choices

Being a leader means making decisions that not everyone will be happy about. A leader cannot make everyone happy. Black Panther upset both his friend W'Kabi and the leader of his army, Okoye, with choices he made about Wakanda. Sometimes you might have to make tough choices that your friends will not like. Here are some examples:

- If you pick someone else to play on your team instead of your friend, in order to be fair.
- If you have to miss a playdate because you have plans with your family.
- If your friend tells you a secret but keeping that secret means somebody could get hurt, you tell a parent or adult.

Black Panther's leadership changed the way the world looked at Wakanda. His kingdom trusted him with its future. When you are a leader, always remember you are making choices for many people. You need to do what is best for them.

BATMAN

BECOMING THE WORLD'S GREATEST

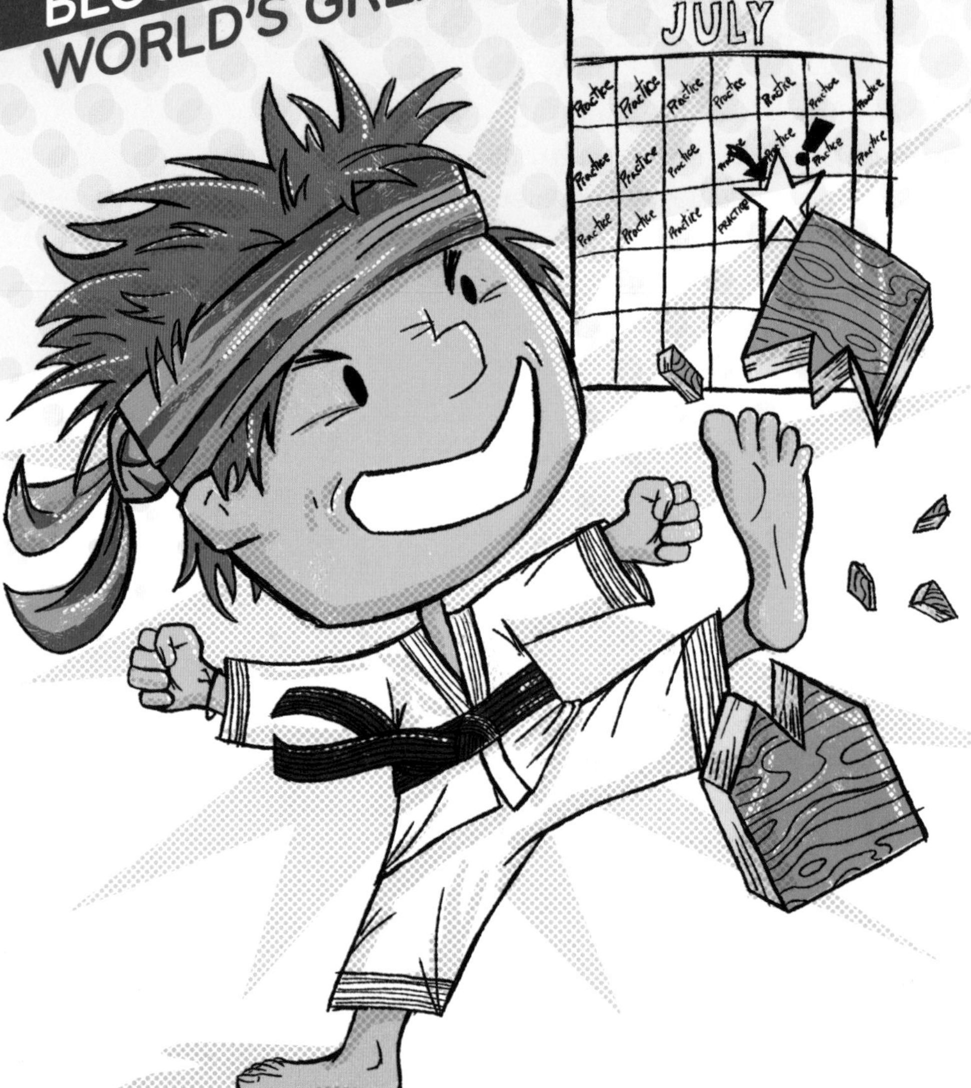

Believing criminals to be superstitious and cowardly, a wealthy orphan sets out to terrify and defeat evildoers in the guise of a bat... but making yourself the world's greatest crime fighter costs more than just money.

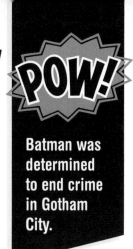

Batman was determined to end crime in Gotham City.

Young Bruce Wayne's life changed forever the night a criminal killed his parents. He swore to avenge them and free Gotham City from all crime. Bruce used his family's great wealth to travel the world. He studied with the best teachers and trained with the best martial arts masters. He returned home smarter and stronger. Just one thing was missing. Bruce needed a way to make criminals fear him. He needed the perfect symbol. One night, a bat crashed through a window into his house. At that moment, Bruce knew he must become Batman. The criminals of Gotham City were about to be in a lot of trouble!

He was ready to do whatever was necessary to fight crime. If you are determined to do something, you can do it. You need to work hard for it. You cannot just put on a mask and cape and call yourself Batman. It takes a lot of effort.

Practice, Practice, and Then Practice More

Whether you want to be a crime fighter or a musician, you need to practice every day. Practice is a major part of having **determination**. Batman never stopped training, even after he became a crime fighter. When he was not patrolling Gotham City, he was home at the Batcave practicing his martial arts and building new crime-fighting gadgets. Training was part of his **routine**.

A routine is something you do often.

Set aside time for yourself to practice. To make the practice part of your routine, try doing it at the same time every day.

Learn from the Best

Your parents, teachers, and coaches all know things that you do not. You should listen to what they have to say. Batman did not think he knew everything. He went looking for teachers. He was one of the world's greatest detectives and greatest fighters because he learned from the best.

Small Battles in a Larger War

Setting goals is an important part of determination. Each small goal will help you move toward a larger one. Batman stopped one crime at a time. One night he stopped the Joker from poisoning Gotham City's water supply. Another night he prevented Two-Face from stealing $2 million from two different banks. Each night a crime was prevented, Batman completed a smaller goal that counted toward his larger goal of ending crime.

BATMAN

If your room is a mess and you think it will be impossible to clean, start with smaller tasks.

- Collect all your dirty clothes and put them in the hamper.
- Pick up all your toys and put them away.
- Sweep or vacuum the floor.
- Scrape the boogers off the wall. (We know the boogers are there. It is a dirty part of the job, but it has to be done.)

Against All Odds

Batman's friend Commissioner Jim Gordon
wanted to know why Batman decided to
fight crime. He asked Batman, "Why did
you have to choose an enemy that's as old
as time and bigger than all of us, Batman?"
"Same reason you did, Jim. I figured I
could take him," Batman told him. The size
of the bad guy did not matter to Batman.
He was going to try to stop him anyway.

Batman's war on crime was an impossible
mission. No one person could ever stop all
crime from happening. But Batman would
keep trying because he was determined
to make a difference. When you are
determined, you will keep trying no matter
how impossible your goal is. You will be
surprised by how much you accomplish.

SPIDER-MAN
A WEB OF RESPONSIBILITY

Bitten by a radioactive spider, a shy teen boy acquires the proportional speed, strength, and agility of a spider…but he soon discovers that having power means having obligations and a duty to help and protect others.

Ouch! Peter Parker felt a surprising sting of pain. A spider bit him as he walked through a science exhibit his class was visiting on a field trip. This spider was not a regular, ordinary spider. It had crawled through one of the science experiments and become radioactive. Peter Parker soon discovered the spider gave him amazing powers, including extra strength and the ability to climb up walls. Peter decided he could use these powers to make money. He made a costume and planned to become rich and famous as Spider-Man. One night after going on a television show, Peter had the chance to stop a robber, but he did not. Sadly, that robber then killed Peter's uncle Ben. Peter learned an important lesson that night – "With great power there must also come great **responsibility**."

SPIDER-MAN

Responsibility means something you are expected to do or a way you are supposed to act.

Spider-Man was not being responsible when he decided to let the robber get away. After his uncle died, Spider-Man said to Iron Man, "When you can do the things that I can, but you don't, and then the bad things happen? They happen because of you." Spider-Man was talking about **consequences**.

There can be good and bad consequences. If you study hard for a quiz, a good consequence would be getting an A on it. There are also bad consequences. If you forget to feed your pet a few times, your parents might decide that you cannot keep it. Spider-Man had a very bad consequence. If Spider-Man had used his powers to stop the robber, his uncle never would have died that night.

Swinging Around the Neighborhood

Not every superhero needs to be out saving the entire planet. When Spider-Man started out, he focused on his neighborhood in Queens, New York. Every neighborhood has its own needs and problems. It is great to think about how to make the whole world better, but do not forget to be responsible for ways to improve your neighborhood. It's where you live so you might as well make it as awesome as you can!

Consequences are the outcome of your actions.

Ways to Help Your Neighborhood

- Participate in food and clothing drives.
- Help out elderly neighbors or volunteer at a nursing home.
- Support nature and wildlife. Make a birdfeeder or grow a butterfly garden.
- Pick up litter to keep streets and sidewalks clean.
- Have a yard or bake sale to raise money for local causes.

Taking Responsibility

An important part of learning responsibility is accepting the bad consequences as well as the good ones. It is easy to say, "It's not my fault," especially if you do not want to get in trouble. You can accept all consequences by taking responsibility.

A Spider-Verse of Responsibility

There's a Spider-Man for every Earth. On one Earth, you'll find Peter Parker. On another you'll find Miles Morales. Gwen Stacy is known as Ghost-Spider on her Earth. And we can't leave out the talking pig Peter Porker, also known as Spider-Ham. Each one of these worlds is different, and that means the heroes have different responsibilities and challenges.

Your friends will have different responsibilities than you do. Maybe you have more chores than they do. Or they spend less time on their homework than you do. It will probably feel unfair. Try not to get distracted by what they are doing. Their world isn't the same, or better or worse, than yours. Keep focused on what you can do. You won't be any less of a Spider-Man if you're doing everything you can to be the best Spider-Man of your own world.

Missing Out Sometimes

Being Spider-Man meant Peter had to occasionally miss out on fun times with his friends. That comes with being responsible. You might not get to go play until your chores are done. You might have to stay home and watch your little brother or sister instead of hanging out with your best friend. It might not seem fair, but it is part of being responsible.

Responsibility gets easier as you grow up. It can feel like a lot as a kid. Spider-Man was only a few years older than you when he took on all his responsibility. If he could handle it, you can, too!

WONDER WOMAN
WARRIOR OF LOVE

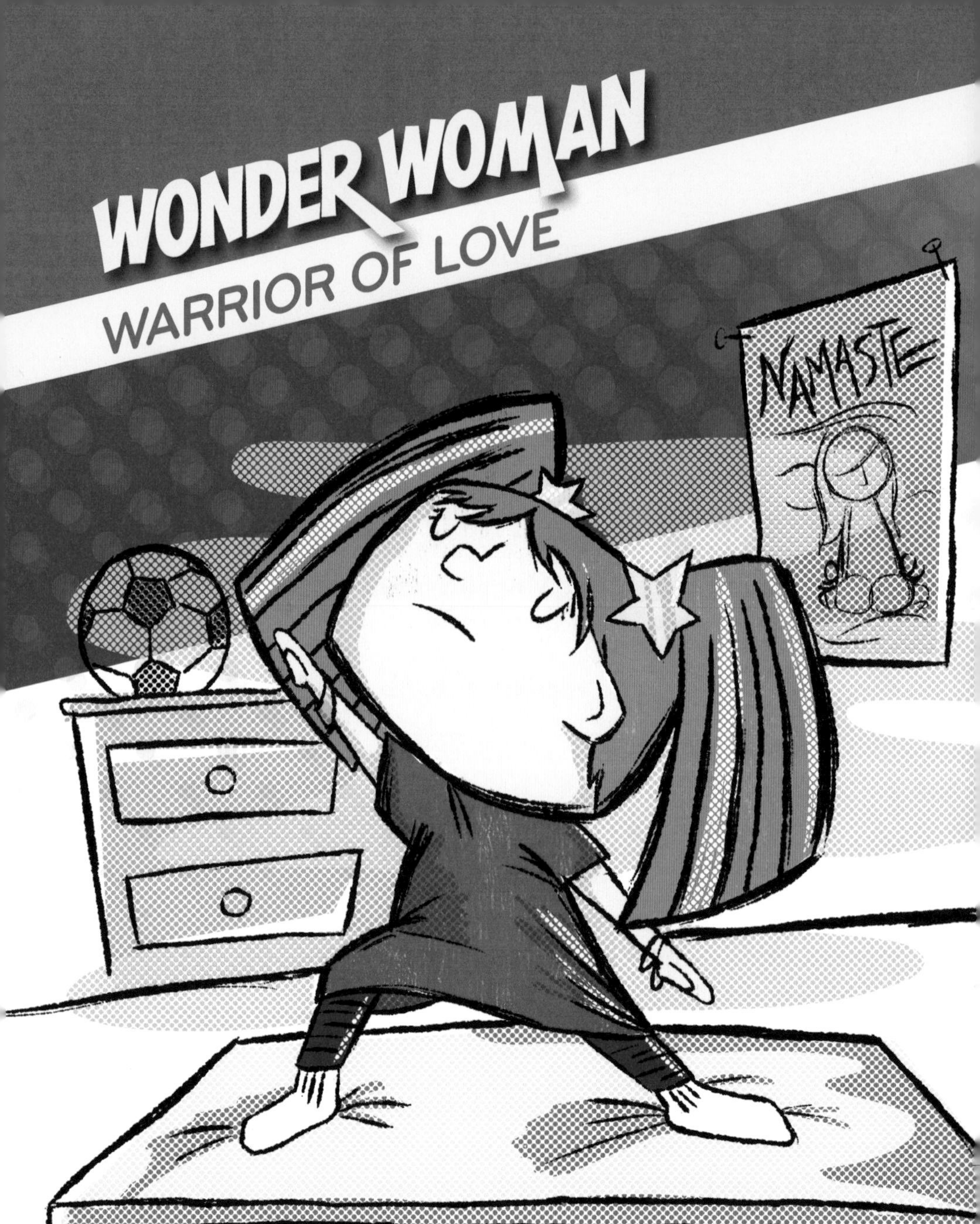
NAMASTE

Hailing from the idyllic Paradise Island of the legendary Amazons, a crusader for peace and understanding journeys to the world of men, where warfare reigns.

On the hidden Paradise Island, Themyscira, the immortal warrior women known as the Amazons lived in peace. Princess Diana was the first and only child born on the island. The Amazons trained her to fight like a warrior, but they also taught her to strive for love and peace above everything else. After army pilot Steve Trevor crashed on the island, Diana won the tournament to decide who would take Trevor home and become the official ambassador of the Amazons. She wanted to promote peace, but she was also prepared for battle with her suit of armor and Golden Lasso of Truth. Her equipment came in handy when Ares, the God of War, attacked. After Diana vanquished Ares with her lasso and saved the day, the press named her Wonder Woman!

33

Why would Wonder Woman train to be a great warrior her entire life if she hoped for peace and not war? She had to protect herself. She was not looking for a fight with Ares, but when he attacked, she was prepared. She was learning self-defense. You might learn self-defense with a martial art like karate or kung fu. You will spend years learning how to protect yourself, but the hardest lesson you will learn is **restraint**.

When you are a warrior like Wonder Woman, you show restraint by not fighting unless you are forced to. Wonder Woman was skilled enough to defeat an entire army with her bare hands, but she would not do that even though she could. She would look for another option first.

The Most Powerful Weapon

Wonder Woman knew that love was greater than any sword or gun. Harmful weapons were used in every war, but Wonder Woman believed, "Only love can truly save the world." Wonder Woman loved everyone and wanted to protect them. Even when she saw people doing horrible things to each other, she showed restraint in two ways:

1) She did not give up on the people.
2) She did not try to fight them.
   She kept loving them.

35

WONDER WOMAN

If someone is mean to you, you can respond with restraint and love like **Wonder Woman** or anger and hate like **Ares.**

WONDER WOMAN

- "That hurt my feelings but I am still your friend."
- "That wasn't nice. Why did you say that?"
- "I'm sorry if I did something to upset you."
- "I hope we can get along."

ARES

- "You're mean. I hate you."
- "Why are you such a jerk?"
- "I'll make you wish you never said that."
- "I'll never speak to you again."

If you are like Wonder Woman, you can bring an end to the fight. If you are like Ares, the fight will likely continue.

Show the World
How Wonderful You Are

Because Wonder Woman was new to the world and because she was a woman, many men thought they could tell her what to do. They did not know about her amazing powers. Sometimes people might think each of you future Wonder Women cannot do something because you are girls. It might make you mad and not want to respond with love.

You should be prepared for times when people treat you this way. You can show restraint by not fighting them, but still using all your strength to prove them wrong. Show them how powerful you are.

CAPTAIN AMERICA
NO PLACE FOR BULLIES

A scrawny kid undergoes a risky experiment to transform himself into a super soldier in order to get to the front lines of war...but the strength to stand up to bullies was always inside him.

Growing up in New York City in the 1930s was hard for Steve Rogers. He was always small and very weak, but that never stopped him from standing up to bullies. When World War II began in Europe, Steve felt it was his duty to join the United States Army and fight the Nazis. There was just one problem. The Army would not let him join because of his weak body. Steve refused to take "no" for an answer and kept trying to join the Army. One day, he was picked for Operation Rebirth, a secret government experiment. Scientists transformed Steve's body with the Super-Soldier Serum. The scrawny boy from New York was now the powerful Captain America. He was ready to go defeat the Nazis!

CAPTAIN AMERICA

Dr. Abraham Erskine, the man who created the Super-Soldier Serum, wanted to know why Steve insisted on joining the Army to fight the Nazis. Steve said to him, "I don't like bullies. I don't care where they're from." Steve believed that bullying was not okay anywhere, from schoolyards to battlefields. He felt so strongly about it that he was willing to do whatever he had to so he could stand up to bullies.

Stay Safe

Always think about your safety. If standing up to a bully seems hard or you do not feel safe, do not do it. Walk away and tell an adult. It is not tattling when dealing with a bully, and you are not weak for getting help.

A Strong Voice

When confronting a bully, speak like
Captain America with all your strength.
Look the bully right in the eyes and tell
them to stop in a calm and strong voice.
Speaking this way is called being **assertive**.

**Being assertive means you are speaking up for
yourself and saying what you need to say.**

Captain America was always a part of a
team. He was a member of the Invaders
in World War II and is a member of the
Avengers today. If you want to confront a
bully but do not want to do it alone, bring
your team. Ask your friends to speak up
with you. One voice telling a bully to stop
is powerful, but many voices saying it
together is even greater.

An Unbreakable Shield

Captain America has a shield to protect him. The shield is made from Vibranium. It cannot be broken. Make your unbreakable shield from something inside you called **confidence**, which can be just as strong as any metal.

You might be feeling angry, scared, or hurt, but you should not show those feelings to the bully. Let the bully's words bounce off your shield of confidence.

Confidence means you believe in yourself and you deserve better than to be bullied.

Your Hero Voice

Here a few things you can say when standing up to a bully:

- "Stop it."
- "I want you to stop that."
- "Knock it off."
- "Give it a rest."
- "I don't like that."
- "Enough!"

Support Your Bullied Friends

Being a good teammate like Captain America also means looking out for others who are bullied. If you see someone who is being bullied, let them know that it is not their fault and they do not deserve it. Promise them they are not alone and make them part of the team.

Since there are all types of bullies, there can be all types of Captain Americas to stand up to them, including you. You do not need the Super-Soldier Serum to be Captain America. You just need the strength to say bullying is wrong.

TEEN TITANS
GO WITH YOUR FRIENDS

A group of teenage superheroes with very little in common other than their ages surprises the world as an awesome new superhero team...but the friendships they form in the group are more triumphant than any victory.

The original Teen Titans were a group of superhero sidekicks who fought crime together away from the grown-up heroes like Batman or Wonder Woman. Months after the team broke up, Robin met the magical Raven. She needed help stopping her demon father, Trigon. Robin and Raven recruited the shape-changing Beast Boy, the alien Starfire, and the half-human/half-machine Cyborg, along with Wonder Girl and Kid Flash from the original team. Together, a new Teen Titans was born. They were a great superhero team, but an even greater group of friends.

TEEN TITANS

Friends Look Out for Each Other

Raven often worried about one day turning evil because of her demonic family. The other Titans promised they would not let that happen. And when Robin decided he no longer wanted to work with Batman and he became a new hero called Nightwing, the Titans cheered him on. When you support your friends, you are showing them you can be **trusted**.

Fighting with Friends

Sometimes friends might hurt your feelings or do something that makes you trust them less. All the Titans were upset when they learned their teammate Terra was lying to them and working as a spy for the villain Deathstroke. If a friend hurts you, you might not want to be friends with them any longer, and that is okay. If they apologize, forgive them. Hopefully you won't discover any of your friends are secretly working for Deathstroke or any other villain.

Trust is the glue that holds friendships together. It is a promise to always have each other's back.

All Types of Friends

The Teen Titans had crime-fighting in common, but each one of them had a very different life and background. For example, Robin grew up as a circus performer. His life was completely different than Starfire's, who was an alien princess. Making your own group of friends will help you see other **points of view**.

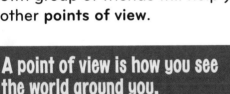

A point of view is how you see the world around you.

You and your friends could have different skin colors and different religions. Some could have big families, and others could have small ones. Some might have a lot of money and live in big houses, and others might not have as much money and live in small apartments. All of these things help shape your point of view. Learning to see your friends' points of view will help you be a better friend.

47

How Silly Can You Be?

You can be as silly as you want to be with your friends. You do not have to behave like you do in the classroom or at the dinner table. Cyborg and Beast Boy loved waffles so much that they decided to play a game to see who could go the longest saying only the word "waffles." Waffles, waffles, waffles. Nothing but waffles! The sign of a great friendship is someone who will be silly with you all day long. Waffles.

No Grown-ups Allowed!

Cyborg's father built the team's headquarters, the high-tech Titans Tower. It was a place where they could hang out and relax. You should have your own private space where you make the rules and you get to decorate.

- Maybe it is a treehouse you can ask your parents to help you build.
- It could also be a fort in your bedroom or closet.
- If you do not have your own space at home, that's okay! You can use a spot on the playground or in a library.

Friendships are like an extra special family because you find each other and decide to be together. If you find a group of friends like the Teen Titans, you will have those friends for life!

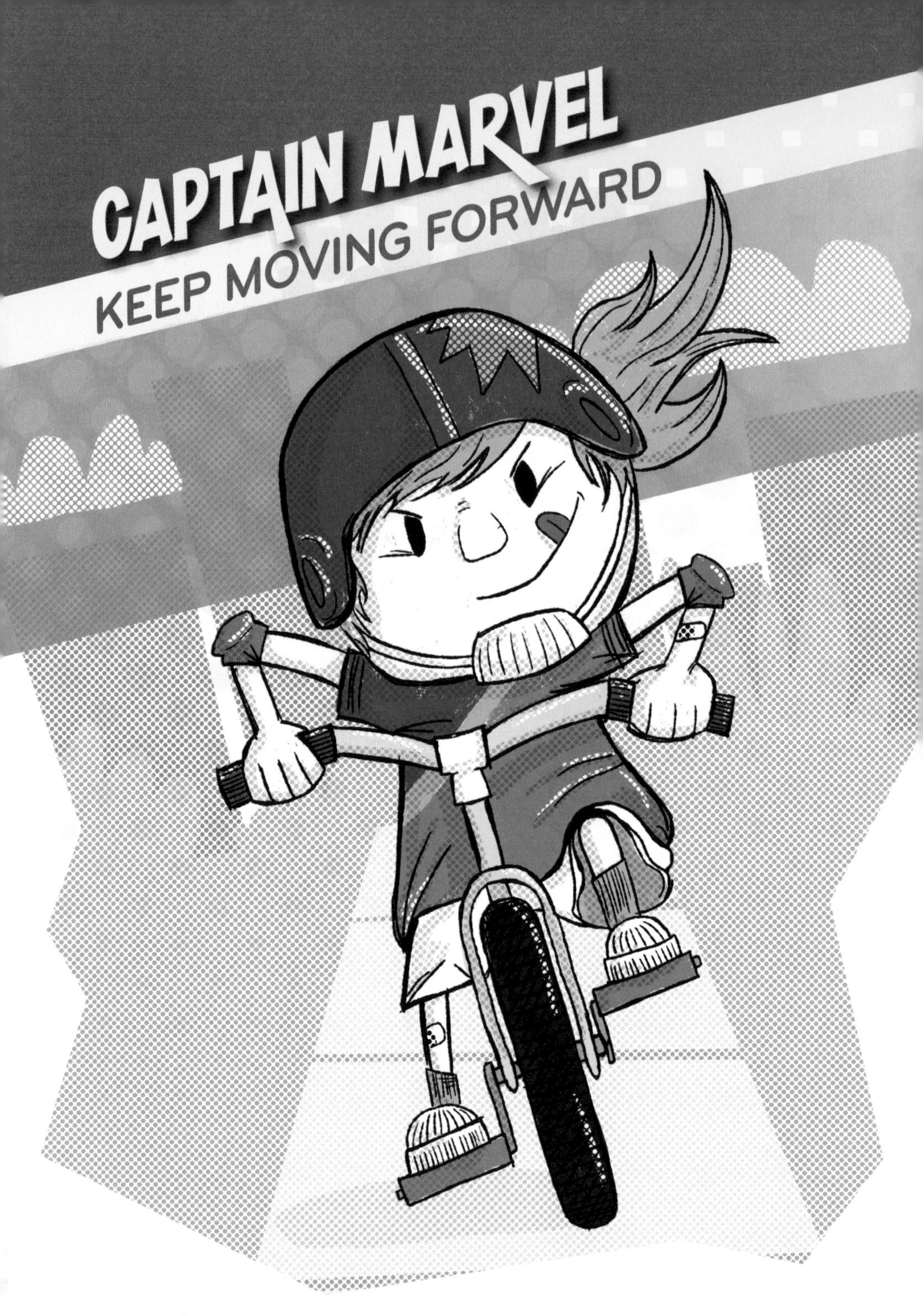
CAPTAIN MARVEL
KEEP MOVING FORWARD

A natural-born flier spends her life fighting to keep what she has and get back what she lost...but it takes true grit, not a rocket ship, to bring her out to space and back.

Air Force pilot Captain Carol Danvers always chased adventures. When she was working at a secret government military base, she became friends with the alien hero Mar-Vell. During a battle between Mar-Vell and the villainous Yon-Rogg, Carol was caught in an explosion from an alien device. She not only survived, but now had superpowers. In honor of her friend, Carol went by the name Ms. Marvel. During her time as a superhero, Carol fought many battles and didn't always win them. She lost her powers and gained new ones. She changed her superhero name with each major change in her life. Carol's adventures took her from Earth to far out in space. When Carol returned to Earth and joined the Avengers, she finally settled on a name. She was the tireless and true fighter known to the world as Captain Marvel!

51

CAPTAIN MARVEL

Captain Marvel had a tough, take-charge attitude. She joked that she liked problems that she could punch. She was the first person to show up to a battle and was the last person standing.

Being great in battle and punching hard did not make her strong. Captain Marvel was strong because she could get back up and keep going after being knocked down. She showed **perseverance** throughout her superhero career.

Captain Marvel was willing to face any obstacle and refused to let defeats stop her. She lost her abilities in a fight with the power-absorbing mutant Rogue. But after a run-in with the evil insect-like aliens the Brood, Carol was transformed into the cosmic-powered Binary and had her many space adventures. She could have given up but she never did.

Perseverance means finding a way to overcome any challenge.

Perseverance Is Stronger Than Any Muscle or Superpower

Perseverance is a feeling inside you that keeps you moving. Here are some examples of perseverance you might have:

- When you fall off your bike and get a bad scrape on your knee, you get right back on the bike.
- When your baseball team is behind, instead of quitting and going home, you step up to the plate and try to hit a homerun.
- When you have trouble learning words for a spelling test, you take a break and then go back to study the words some more.
- When you lose to the big boss in a video game ten times, you restart the level and try again.

Bouncing Back

Yon-Rogg returned to Earth with plans of destroying New York City at a time when Captain Marvel's powers were damaging her brain. Her friends and doctors told her not to fly so she would not get hurt more. She fought Yon-Rogg anyway and saved New York City. In the final battle, she lost most of her memories. Instead of quitting being a superhero, Captain Marvel went back out on another mission with the Avengers to save Earth. She was **resilient**. Captain Marvel's missing memories were not going to stop her when Earth was in danger. She went back out to space to get the mission done.

Being resilient means you bounce back quickly from something hard.

Keep Going!

You might lose a sports game or not do as well as you wanted on a test. Do not let that loss stop you from trying again. Captain Marvel's motto was "Higher, Further, Faster, More." After every setback, try a little bit harder instead of getting stuck. You will fly higher, go further, move faster, and succeed more. If you have perseverance like Captain Marvel and you can be as resilient as she is, there will be no limit to all the great things you will do

SWAMP THING

MAKE YOUR WORLD A LITTLE GREENER

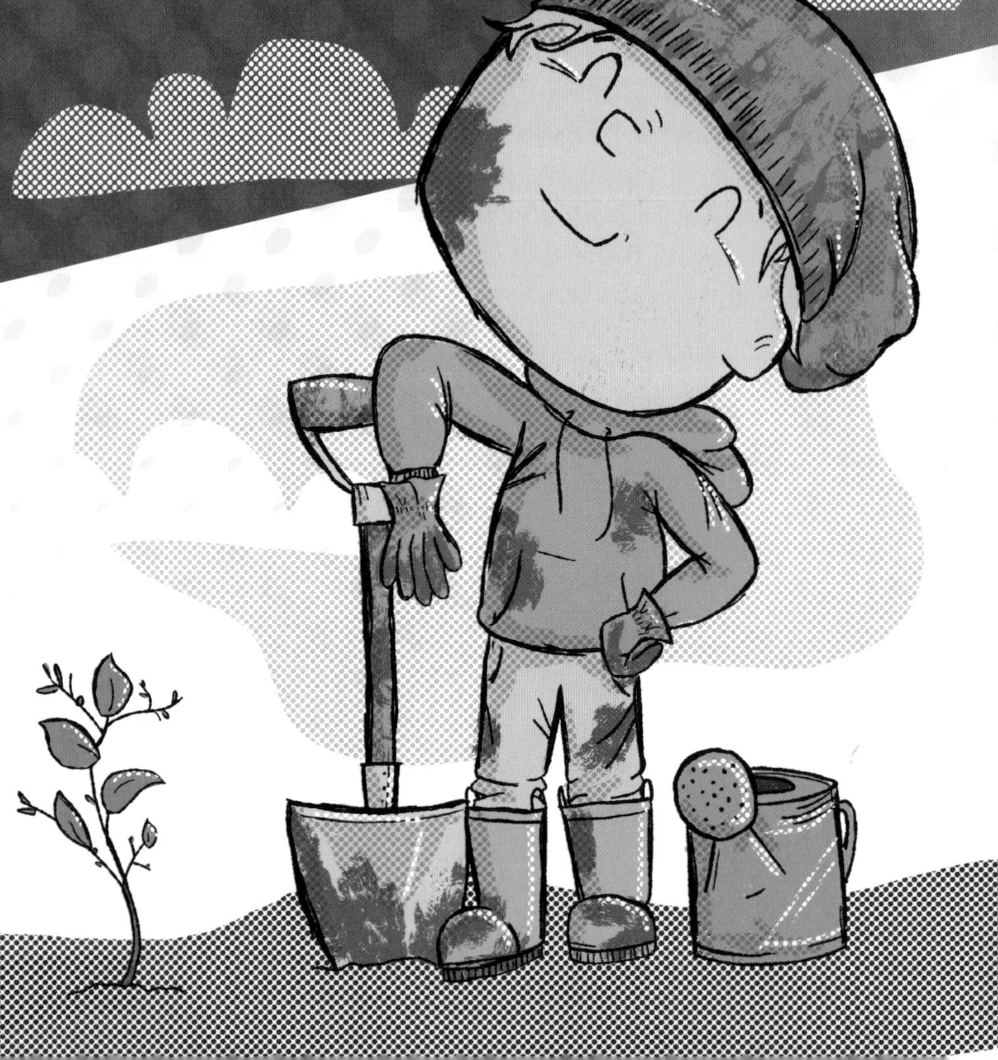

A scientist's connection to the natural world grows deeper when he is transformed into a plant creature who dwells in the Louisiana swamps. With his power to control plant life comes the burden of protecting all living things.

ZAP!

The environment is everything in nature, including humans, animals, and plants.

Plants are living things. But there is no plant like Swamp Thing! The monstrous green creature came to life the night a scientist named Alec Holland was caught in a laboratory explosion. Alec's body was covered in chemicals from his experiments when he fell into the swamp. He died in those swampy waters, but thanks to the chemicals, he was reborn as Swamp Thing! The creature had a great mission. With the power to control all plant life in the world, Swamp Thing was in charge of protecting the **environment** from anyone who would try to harm it.

When Swamp Thing defended plant life, he was actually protecting all life. Plants produce the air we breathe. We would not be alive without them.

57

SWAMP THING

Make Every Day Earth Day

Swamp Thing could regrow entire forests in minutes. Since we do not have his powers, it will take a little bit longer for us. Many people plant trees on Earth Day, but you do not have to wait until then to get started. Every tree you plant will provide more oxygen to breathe.

Threats to the Environment

Swamp Thing battled both evil supernatural forces and ordinary humans looking to do harm. Here are some of the biggest threats our planet is facing today:

Pollution: There are many types of pollution that can affect our air, soil, and water.

Climate Change: The world is getting hotter, causing ice caps to melt, crops to die, and other problems.

Deforestation: Forests are being cut down to make room for cities or farms, or for the wood to be sold.

If these threats are not stopped, the world might not be able to sustain life in the future—no humans, no animals, no plants, and no Swamp Things. It could be a big, empty planet!

59

SWAMP THING

The Three R's

Pollution can weaken Swamp Thing's powers in addition to harming our planet. The best way to help prevent pollution is by learning and following the three R's.

Reduce: Look for ways to cut back on the amount of waste you and your family create.

Reuse: Instead of throwing things away, look for other uses for them.

Recycle: Separate your glass, plastic, and paper instead of throwing it in the garbage so it can go to the local recycling center.

Swamp Thing has a special connection to the environment that makes him aware of all the dangers that could harm it. You can have that connection, too, by learning about threats to the environment and ways to stop them. We only have this one planet. We all need to protect it like Swamp Thing.

Talking to Plants

Swamp Thing can communicate with all plants through the Green, a force that connects plant life throughout the planet. You cannot have a conversation with plants, but they can still tell you a lot of things.

- Change in seasons: In spring, leaves start to grow on trees. In summer, the leaves are full blooms of green. In fall, the leaves turn red, yellow, and orange. In winter, the trees appear dead.
- Watering time: Plants start to wilt when they need water. It is their way of saying they are thirsty.
- A natural compass: Moss grows mostly on the same side of trees and rocks. Once you learn how to identify it, you can determine which way is north.
- Names and warning signs: The shapes and colors of leaves on a plant or tree can tell you what kind it is. For example, if you see groups of three pointy-tipped leaves on a vine, you can know that it is poison ivy and you should stay away.
- Some people believe talking to plants can actually help them grow. Even though it is hard to prove, it does not hurt to try!

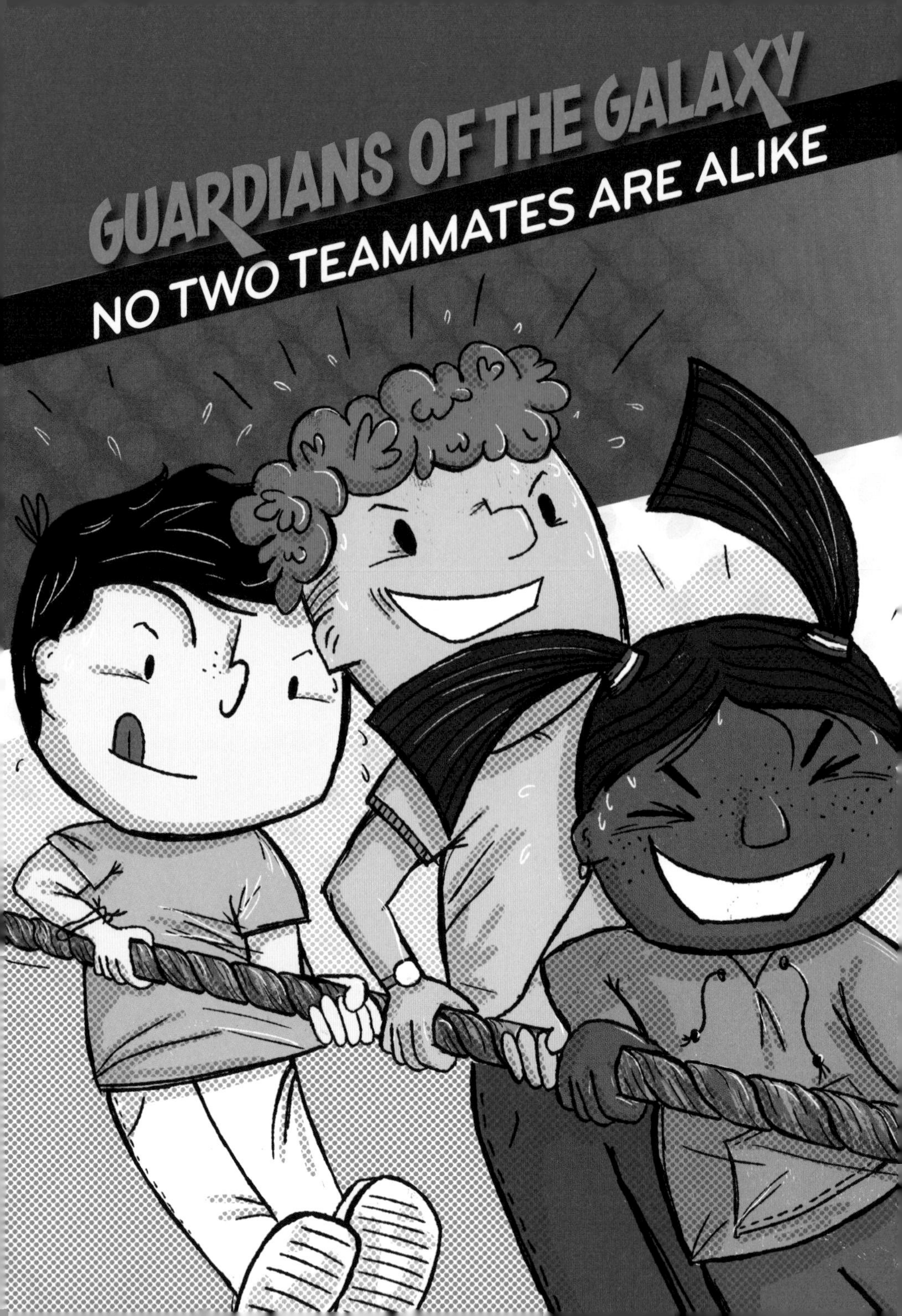
GUARDIANS OF THE GALAXY
NO TWO TEAMMATES ARE ALIKE

The unlikeliest team of heroes somehow manages to work together and save the galaxy time and time again. They may look different from you and from each other…but when a threat arises, they've got what it takes.

What a lineup! The sarcastic and sometimes selfish Star-Lord used to be a space pirate. Gamora was a master assassin for her adopted father, the evil Thanos. The hard-headed Drax was a warrior out for revenge against Thanos for murdering his family. The furry Rocket Raccoon was a genius with weapons but he was also angry and untrusting because of the brutal experiments that made him smart. And then there was Groot, the living tree who only ever said, "I am Groot." What do you get when you put these individuals on a spaceship together? The Guardians of the freaking Galaxy, as Rocket might say. You would never expect this team to save the day, and that is what made them so special.

If you had a young Groot in your classroom, you might want to ask, "What's wrong with that tree-boy?" It is okay to be curious and want to know why he only ever says, "I am Groot." Everybody is different, but sometimes those differences are more noticeable. It is important to treat everyone with kindness and respect, no matter how different they are.

If you are nervous about talking to somebody who is different, here is a tip: Just smile and say hello.

Find What You Have in Common

Even though Groot cannot say more than three words, he can still do many amazing things, like the way he can grow his body. If you only see a person's major difference, you might miss all the many other great things about them. You also might not learn about the things you have in common, like how Groot enjoys a lot of the same music as Star-Lord. You could miss out on a great friendship if you avoid people with differences.

Having patience means not getting upset if you have to wait on someone or something that takes extra time.

Giving Guardians Their Time

Drax often says whatever he's thinking, even if it's not appropriate. He does not know that what he's saying is inappropriate and sometimes hurts other people's feelings. If you have a friend like Drax, you probably need to have a little extra **patience** with them.

Gamora did not show patience when she told Drax and the rest of the team that they were idiots. Friends like Drax might not understand what you are saying. They might not get your jokes. They definitely might not understand why you think what they said is funny or inappropriate. The more time you spend together, the more you both will learn how to best talk to each other.

Rocket was not always very nice to people with physical differences. He liked to take their robotic legs or eyes because he thought it was funny. Mocking people with physical differences is never okay, and Rocket was wrong to do it. Do not make the same mistake Rocket did.

How to Treat Your New Teammates When Seeing Someone Different:

- Do not point and stare.
- Do not make fun.
- Do not be mean.

Not everyone looks and talks like Superman or Black Panther, but that does not mean they cannot be superheroes. The Guardians of the Galaxy proved that, every time they faced a threat like Ronan or Ego. They are a great team because of their differences. More importantly, each person is welcome in the group. Anyone can be a Guardian of the Galaxy.

GREEN LANTERN CORPS

SHINING A NEW LIGHT IN THE UNIVERSE

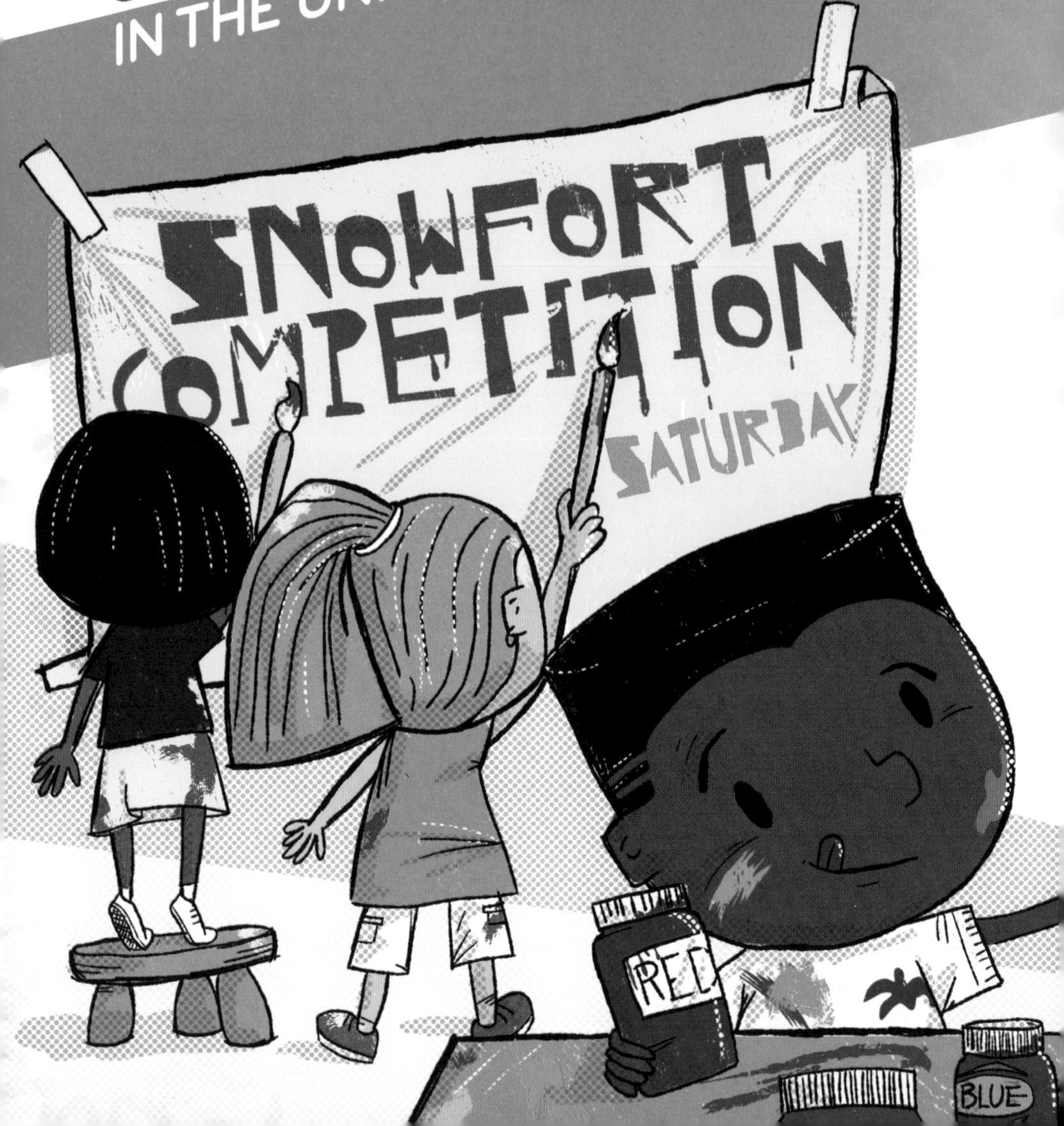
SNOWFORT
COMPETITION
SATURDAY
RED
BLUE

The most powerful weapon in the universe is small enough to fit on your finger. In order to join the ranks of those who wield it, a person must overcome great fear and let their imagination run wild.

The universe is very large, with more planets and life-forms than you could ever count. There are just as many dangers. The ancient and wise Guardians of the Universe formed the Green Lantern Corps to patrol the universe like police officers and protect it. Each Green Lantern wore a power ring that could create solid objects called constructs from whatever the person imagined. If the person was afraid, the ring would not work. Some Green Lanterns came from Earth, like the pilot Hal Jordan and the marine John Stewart, as well as newer members like Simon Baz and Jessica Cruz. No two Green Lanterns were alike. They were each special in the Green Lantern Corps and used their rings in **creative** ways.

When you have a ring that can make anything, being creative is your greatest strength. Learning to be creative means flexing your brain like a muscle when a problem comes up, even if you are not battling bad guys in space.

Creativity Comes in Different Shapes and Sizes

Everyone can be creative in their own way. Do not compare yourself to others.

Hal Jordan liked to make large constructs with his ring, swatting bad guys away with a giant fist or baseball bat. John Stewart's constructs were always very detailed. You could see every nut and bolt that went into making them. What would your constructs look like?

Overcoming Fear

Fear was the greatest weakness of a Green Lantern, and it can ruin creativity. Jessica Cruz was one of the newest Green Lanterns. She struggled a lot with fear. Her fear kept her from being able to make solid constructs with her ring.

Her partner, Simon Baz, battled with fear, too. He carried a gun to protect himself because he feared his ring might not work one day. He doubted his own strength and feared the ring could fail him.

Both Jessica and Simon had to learn how to deal with their fears to become better Green Lanterns. Any expert Green Lantern will tell you that being fearless is impossible. Success comes from working through that fear.

Mistakes Are Not Failure

Each mistake you make is a chance to let fear sneak back in and grab hold of you. You have to fight that. Fear nearly defeated John Stewart after he failed to save the planet Xanshi from destruction. He was ready to give up being a Green Lantern. Instead, he worked through the fear, which made him an even greater Green Lantern. John even became the leader of the Green Lantern Corps. Mistakes are not failure. Failure is giving up and not trying again because you are afraid.

Once you've mastered being creative and overcoming fear, you will be as powerful as any member of the Green Lantern Corps. There will be nothing you cannot create.

Creative Workouts

You can improve your creativity in many ways:

- **Daydream** – Have you ever heard the expression "having your head in the clouds"? That is a good place to be since you can look down on everything going on. Let your mind wander.
- **Experiment** – From mixing paints to create new colors to banging on a piano to find a melody, experimenting can lead to great and unexpected results.
- **Play** – Having fun and playing gives your brain a good workout, so keep on playing with your Legos, Minecraft, guessing games, and puzzles.
- **Perform** – Make your own movie or a puppet show or read a poem you wrote. Tell a story any way you like.
- **Innovate** – Think of ways to make life better and easier. Would you invent a spice that made veggies taste like candy? How about shoes with laces that always stayed tied? Start small and go big. How about a special kind of magnet that could pull all the plastic garbage out of the ocean?

MS. MARVEL

BE SURE TO STRETCH

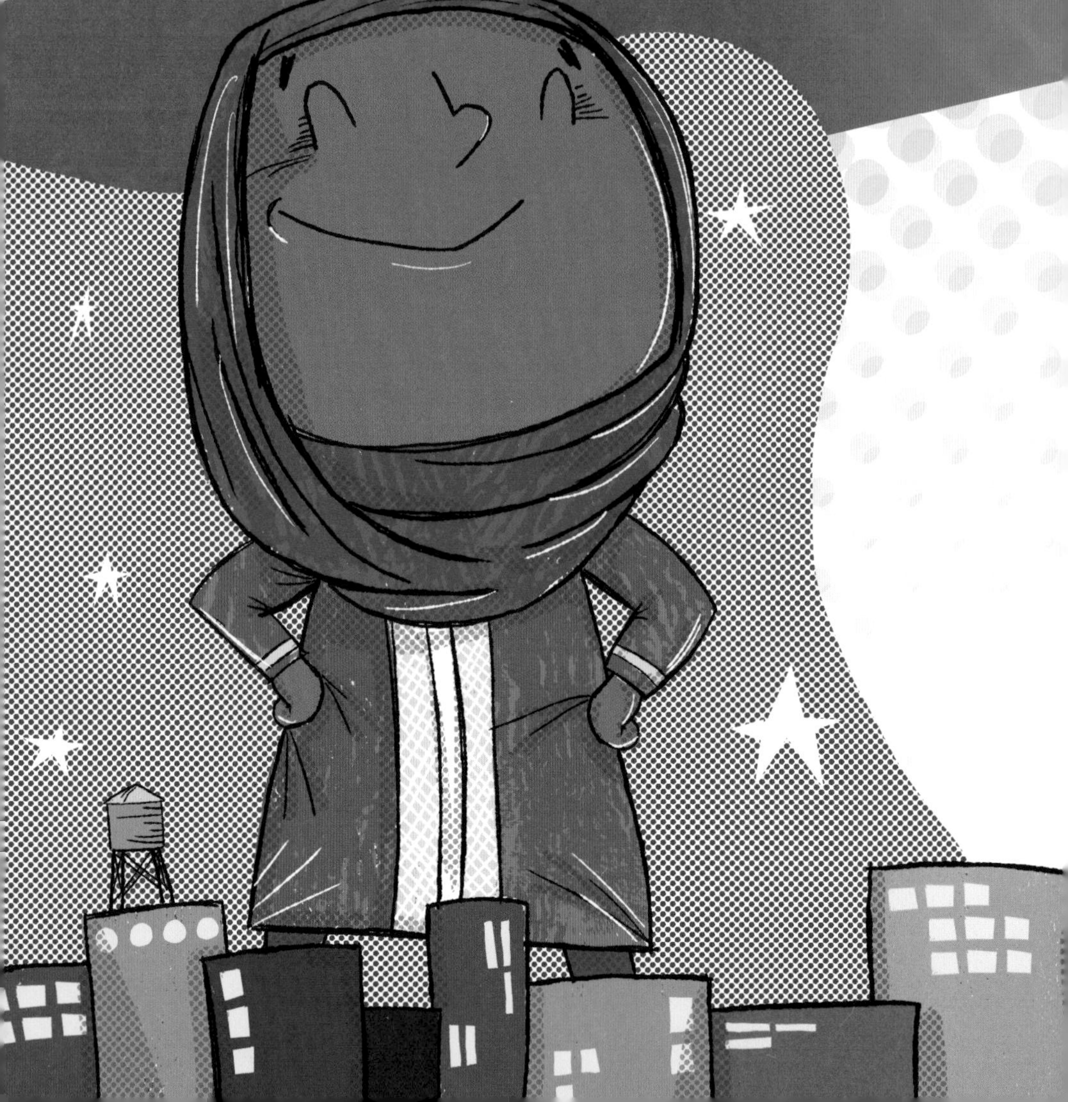

A twist of fate grants an ordinary teenage girl the gift to change her body in many different and fantastic ways...but being flexible and adaptable doesn't solve all her problems. Growing up doesn't just mean getting bigger.

Kamala Khan was a normal teen struggling to fit in at home with her strict Muslim parents and at school, where people made fun of the nerdy things she liked. As if Kamala did not have enough problems to deal with, she learned she was actually an Inhuman! When she was exposed to the Terrigen Mist, a gas that activates super-powered Inhuman DNA, she developed special abilities. All of a sudden, Kamala could make her body really big, stretch herself way out, and even take on the appearance of other people. She decided to use her abilities to protect her hometown, Jersey City, from evil. Since her idol Carol Danvers was no longer using the name Ms. Marvel, Kamala decided to take it. Her life got a lot crazier, but Ms. Marvel was ready for the challenge.

MS. MARVEL

Ms. Marvel's powers let her twist and stretch her body in many different ways, which made her an excellent addition to superhero teams like the Avengers and the Champions. She was incredibly **flexible**. You do not need an elastic body like Ms. Marvel's to be flexible.

Flexible means being able to stretch and bend, but it also means you are okay with things changing.

You might have planned a fun day at the park. Then it starts to rain that morning and you cannot go. It is sad and frustrating because you were looking forward to it. Instead of getting too upset, you can find a way to have a fun day inside. That is being flexible!

Kamala had to get used to a lot of change once she became Ms. Marvel.

Another Way of Being Flexible Is Being Open to New Things

- When your parents ask you to try a food you do not think you will like
- When your friends have different rules for a game you all like to play
- When your teacher wants you to try solving a math problem a different way

She had many new challenges on top of school and her family. The world of superheroes was brand new to her, but she jumped right in!

Embiggen Yourself!

Ms. Marvel liked to shout "embiggen" and grow really big, even as big as a house! One way for you to grow is to **be the bigger person** in a disagreement with friends or siblings.

Being the bigger person means letting the other person have their way.

Ms. Marvel definitely had to be the bigger person with her brother Aamir sometimes, even though he was older. Even if you know you are right and they are wrong, it is sometimes better to end a disagreement. Then you can get back to the fun stuff.

Don't Wear Yourself Out!

Kamala could heal quickly when she was injured, but only when she did not use any of her other powers. Sometimes she had to not be Ms. Marvel just so she could heal completely.

You should always take time for yourself. It is great to stretch yourself, but try not to stretch yourself too thin. School, family, and friends can tire you out even when everything is great. Use private, quiet time to relax and recharge your body and your mind. Otherwise you might be flopping around like loose socks that lost their elastic stretch!

When You Can Be Anyone, Be Yourself

Before Ms. Marvel got her powers, she really wanted to fit in with the cool kids at school, even though they were not very nice to her. She thought they were normal and she was not. Once Ms. Marvel had her powers and could change her appearance, she discovered it was exhausting to pretend to be someone else. It was not fun, and it did not make her happy.

Just because you are flexible enough to twist yourself into something you are not, that does not mean you should. Instead of trying to be someone else, be the best version of yourself that you can be. That is what Kamala did as Ms. Marvel!

CYBORG
BUILDING YOURSELF BACK UP

A teen with many natural athletic abilities suffers a tragedy that leaves much of his body badly damaged. His father replaces his injured body parts with advanced cybernetic machinery. Now he has a new potential for greatness... if only he can see past the things he is missing.

Victor Stone was a star high school athlete and hoped to become a professional athlete one day. He did not want to be a scientist like his parents. One night, an explosion in his mother's laboratory killed her and nearly killed Victor, too. Victor's father raced to save his son's life. Most of Victor's body was destroyed. His father replaced those parts with advanced machinery. He was now Cyborg, half human and half robot. Instead of being happy to be alive, Victor was angry. He thought he looked like a freak and did not like the way people seemed to be afraid of him. When Cyborg used his new abilities to stop a terrorist attack at the United Nations, he learned he could be a hero, even if he still did not feel normal.

CYBORG

Who Do You See in the Mirror?

Cyborg called himself a monster and tried to hide his face under a hood, which is a pretty negative **body image**.

Cyborg Was a Strong and Smart Hero but Still Had Problems with His Self-Esteem.

- If you love and respect yourself, you have high self-esteem.
- If you only think negative things about yourself, you have low self-esteem.
- Low self-esteem can pull you down like an anchor and hold you back from doing great things.

A positive body image means you feel good about the way you look and the things your body can do. You are not worried that you are not tall enough, or good-looking enough, or skinny enough. With a positive body image, you know you are perfect exactly the way you are.

Self-esteem is how you feel about yourself.

Body image is one part of self-esteem. It is how you feel about how you look and how you think others see you.

CYBORG

Your "Best" List

One way to build your self-esteem is to list all the positives about yourself. Cyborg's body could do some amazing things. In addition to super strength and built-in jets for flying, he could connect to any computer and process information super fast. He could also transform parts of his body, like making his arm into a sonic cannon. His "Best" list was really long!

What would be on your "Best" list? Pick five things you like the most about yourself and write them down.

If having a sonic cannon for an arm is on your list, too, we need to have a talk.

Titans Good, Street Gang Bad

Cyborg was lucky to find a group of friends in the Teen Titans, but he was not always so lucky. Even before he became Cyborg, he had self-esteem issues. He did not feel good fighting with his parents all the time about playing sports. A friend at the time was Ron, a kid in a street gang. Ron did not help him feel good about himself. They only got in trouble together. Friends like Ron will not help your self-esteem. They will not help you focus on positive things. And when you are stuck thinking negative things about yourself, it will be hard to help your self-esteem.

No one can give you positive self-esteem. You have to find it in yourself. Cyborg did, and it allowed him to become a great superhero. He grew up to lead a new group of Teen Titans, and he also graduated to a spot in the Justice League.

IRON MAN

SHARE YOUR POWER

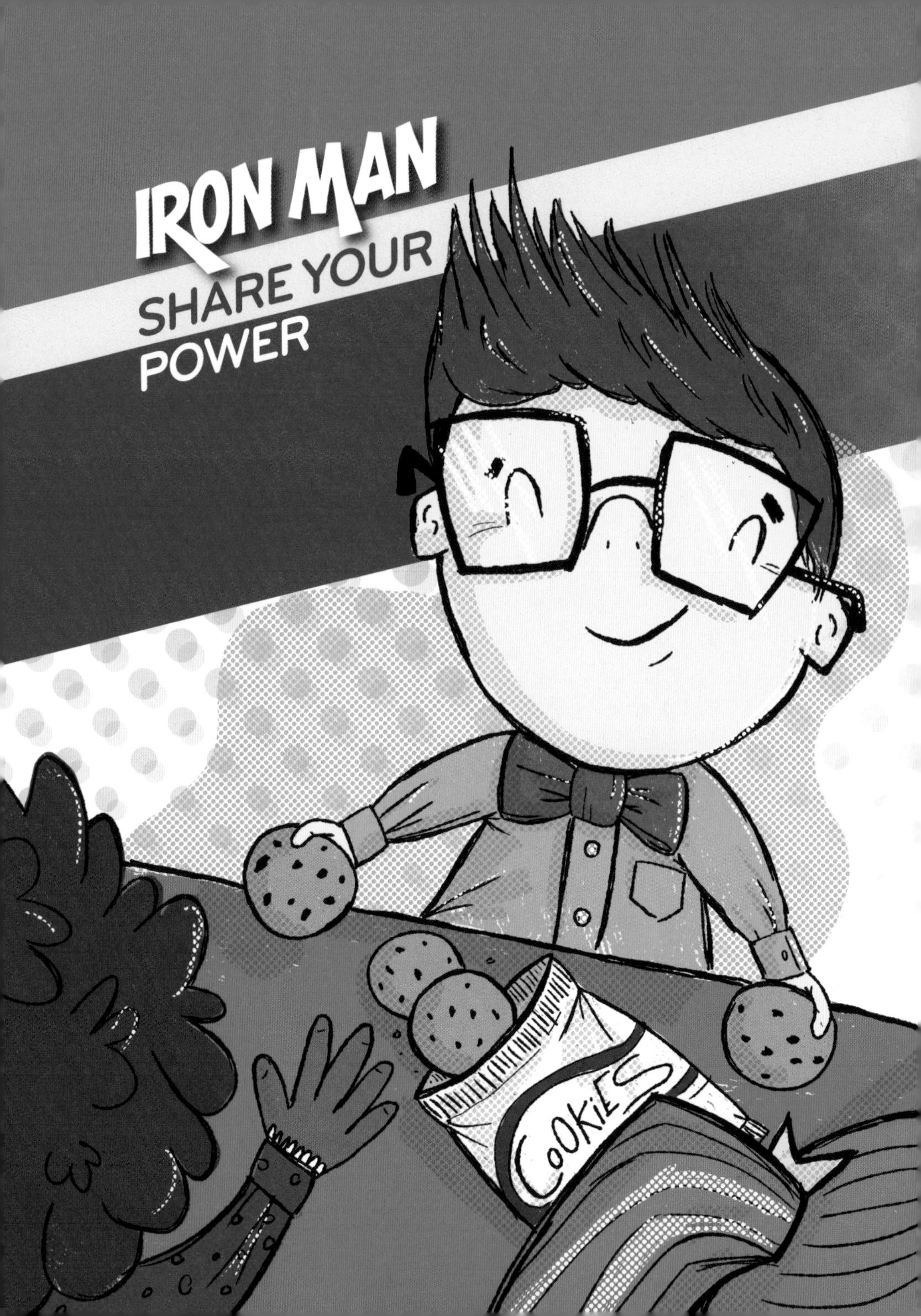
COOKIES

A genius inventor used his brains to make money rather than help the world. After a life-changing experience he barely survived, he's ready to use his inventions to help the world and to share them with others.

Tony Stark was one of the smartest people in the world. For most of his life, he used those smarts to invent weapons of war he could sell for lots of money. One day while showing his latest invention, Tony was severely injured and kidnapped by terrorists. They wanted him to build weapons they could use. Instead, Tony built a metal suit to keep himself alive and escape. After he escaped, Tony could not go back to selling weapons. He kept improving his suit, which he wore as Iron Man! He used his great intelligence and all his money to protect and help the world. He paid for everything the Avengers needed and worked on inventions that would do good instead of harm.

87

IRON MAN

Before Tony Stark became Iron Man, he was **selfish**.

Tony did not think about what other people needed or wanted. He would not do anything that did not benefit him in some way. A selfish person will not have many friends.

Selfish means you only care about yourself.

The opposite of selfish is **selfless**, and that is exactly what Tony became as Iron Man.

Iron Man was also very generous, meaning he was willing to give to others. Iron Man was able to do a lot with his money, like building a headquarters for the Avengers.

Sharing Your Gifts

Iron Man's powerful technology allowed him to save the day again and again. In addition to using his inventions himself, he also shared what he invented with others. He gave his friend Colonel James "Rhodey" Rhodes a suit. As War Machine, Rhodey joined Iron Man in many battles, both as partners and with the Avengers. Iron Man also gave some of his technology to Riri Williams, a teenage genius who built her own suit and became Ironheart. By sharing what he invented, Iron Man was sharing his knowledge with others.

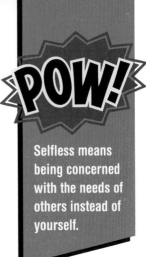

Selfless means being concerned with the needs of others instead of yourself.

What Can You Give?

You do not need lots and lots of money to be selfless and generous. You can do it in the tiniest of ways and still make a difference.

- Donate old toys and clothing during a collection drive.
- Play what your friends want to play even if you would rather play something else.
- Share your dessert.
- Make someone a gift.

89

IRON MAN

Knowledge is a wonderful gift to share with others. If you are great at a subject in school like math or English and have a friend who struggles with the subject, you should offer to help them. When you do your homework together, you can try to explain the things they do not understand.

Your Power Source

Tony Stark loved being Iron Man. It was thrilling to fight bad guys and save the world. Do you want to know a little about being a superhero? It feels fantastic to help others! It is one of the best feelings in the world, and you will want to keep doing it.

Iron Man invented the Arc Reactor to power his suit, but the power you need to keep helping will come from seeing all the good you do. Making other people's lives better any way you can will feel wonderful! You will want to keep doing it, just like Iron Man.

BATWOMAN

BE TRUE TO YOURSELF

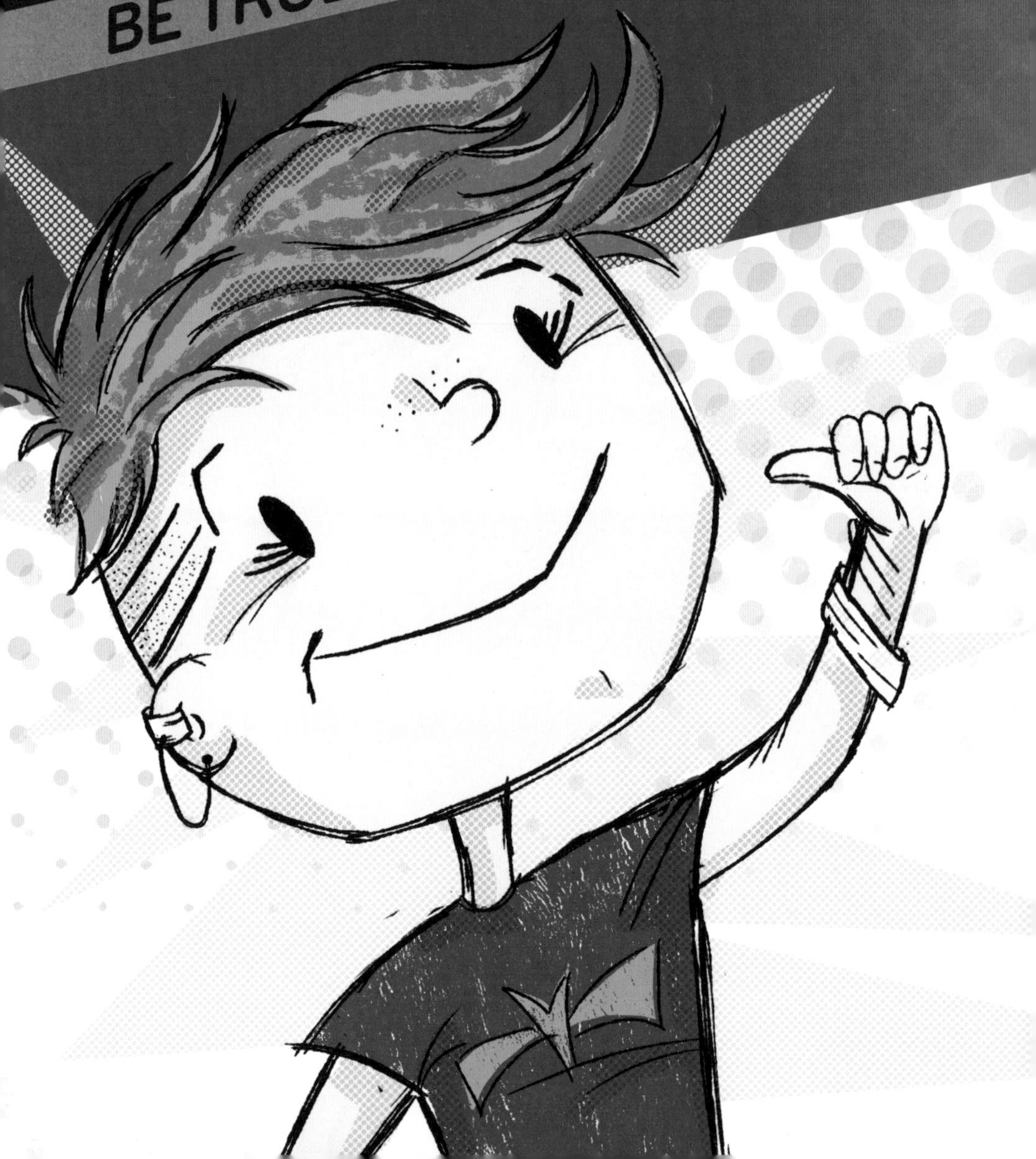

A passionate and dedicated woman gives up on her dream to serve in the Army because it means lying about who she is. She finds another way to serve and redefines what the bat symbol can mean in the fight to do good.

Kate Kane wanted to serve in the U.S. Army ever since she was a child. She was a top student at the United States Military Academy, but one day she decided to quit. If Kate wanted to be in the Army, she needed to lie about being a lesbian. Kate refused to do that and gave up on her future in the military. She looked for another way to serve and do good. She found the inspiration she needed the night Batman rescued her from a mugger. If Kate could not wear an Army uniform, she'd wear the bat symbol. Her father, Colonel Jacob Kane, did not want Kate to become a vigilante like Batman, but he helped train her when it was clear she would not change her mind. Kate became Batwoman!

BATWOMAN

BATWOMAN

> **Having integrity means doing what is right because it is the right thing to do, even if it is hard to do.**

Batwoman showed she had **integrity** when she chose to leave the Army instead of lying to hide that she was a lesbian.

She could have very easily lied and not been caught, but it was more important to her to do the right thing. Sometimes having integrity means giving up something important to you, like Batwoman did when she quit military school. Becoming Batwoman allowed her to keep her integrity and still serve justice.

Question Authority

Colonel Kane did not always have the same integrity his daughter did. He ran a secret military group called the Colony. The Colony was formed to stop the evil League of Shadows. Colonel Kane was ready to do anything to destroy the League of Shadows, even if innocent people died in the battle. Batwoman believed killing innocent people was wrong. She stopped her father with the help of Batman and other heroes. Batwoman was not afraid to **question the authority** of her father when he was going to let people die.

Testing Your Integrity

It is easy to tell right from wrong, but being able to act the right way shows you have integrity.

Ask yourself:

- If you saw someone drop a $20 bill on the ground, would you keep it for yourself instead of returning it?
- If you saw someone else's answers to a test, would you copy them if the teacher was not looking?
- If your friends thought it would be fun to steal candy from a store, would you join them?

Batwoman would say "no" to all three questions because she has integrity. And if you answered "yes" to any of these things, Batwoman might need to pay you a visit.

It is okay to question authority as long as you are acting with integrity. If you have a concern but are not sure if you should question authority, just ask politely, share your concern with your parent or teacher, and be willing to listen to what they say.

Having integrity like Batwoman means you will have to make hard choices. You might not always be happy with those choices, but you will be doing the right thing. That sort of integrity is what earns you a bat symbol on your chest.

Making the Call:
When is it okay to question authority?

Question: One of your parents never looks both ways before crossing the street. Do you say something?

Answer: Yes! Everyone should follow safety rules.

Question: Is it okay to tell your teacher you think you are getting too much homework because you do not like doing it every night?

Answer: Nope. Stop trying to get out of doing your homework.

Question: Your parents tell you that you cannot watch a movie because it is too grown-up for you. Do you watch it anyway when they are not around?

Answer: No. Your parents are looking out for you and are good judges of what is appropriate to watch.

Question: There is a food fight in the lunchroom and the wrong kid is being sent to the principal for starting it. Can you tell your teacher they made a mistake?

Answer: Yes. You are sticking up for someone and being honest.

HULK
SMASH YOUR ANGER

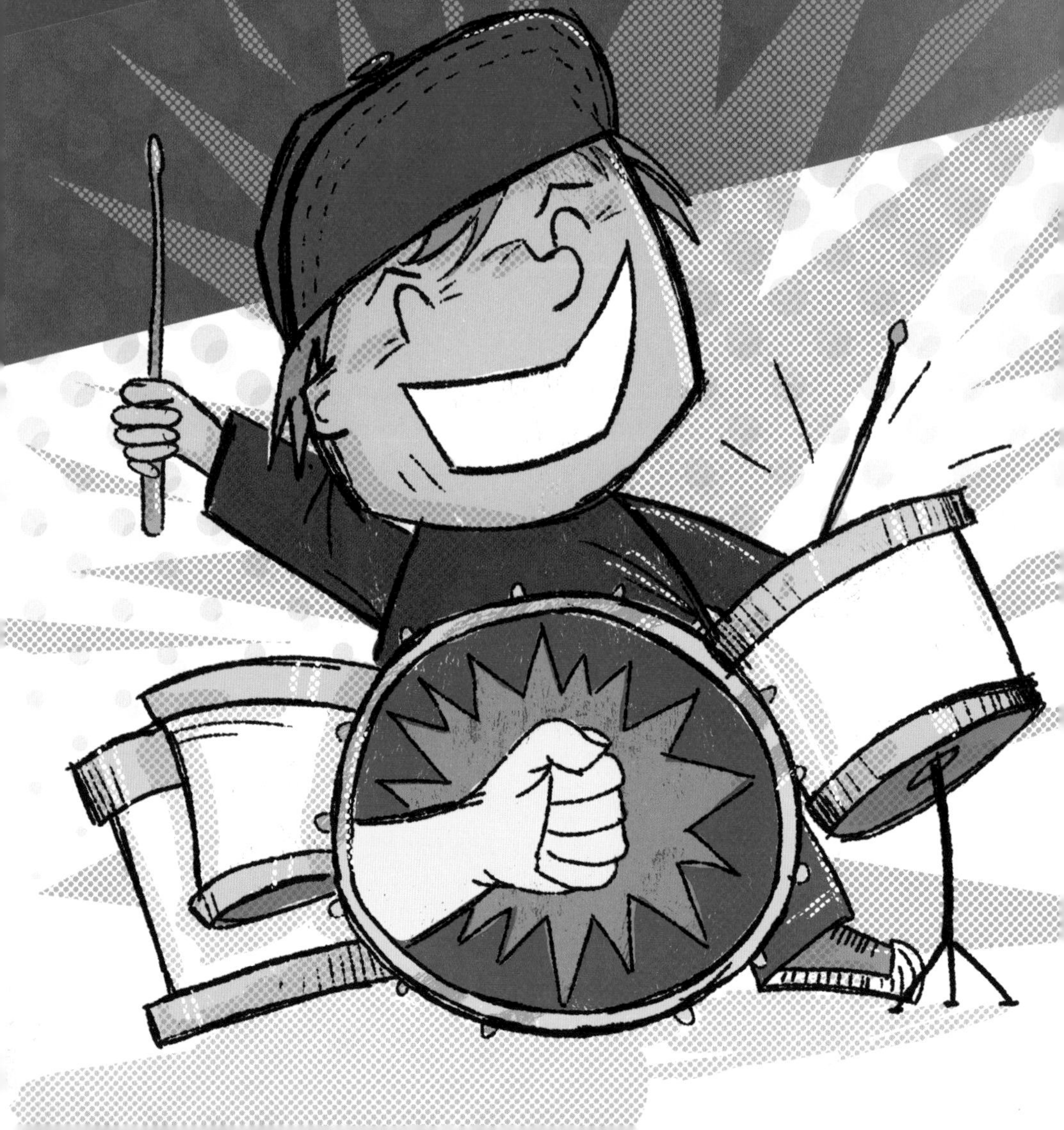

A freak accident causes a scientist to transform into a raging beast whenever he gets angry. He dedicates his life to finding a cure...but anger is the toughest monster to tame.

Scientist Bruce Banner should have died after an experiment gone wrong exposed him to a dangerous amount of gamma radiation. At first, he appeared completely unharmed. But a short time later, Bruce discovered that he turned into the monstrous Hulk when he got angry. The big green monster was powered by rage and only ever had one thing on his mind—smashing things! Bruce could not control himself when he was the Hulk. Even after Hulk joined the Avengers, his rage was uncontrollable and caused a lot of damage. Bruce spent years looking for a cure to stop himself from becoming the Hulk but did not find one. During that time, though, he got better at controlling his emotions. It did not always prevent him from becoming the Hulk, but it helped stop some of his destruction.

HULK

Getting angry is perfectly normal. It happens to everyone. And you do not have to get caught in a gamma experiment to cause your anger to make you want to smash things like Hulk.

Early Warning Signs

Bruce had early warning signs when he started to turn into the Hulk, like a faster heartbeat and his eyes turning green. When you know your warning signs, you can better control your anger.

What Color Is Your Hulk?

Hulk is known for being green. But did you know that other times he turned grey? And there's a whole different character called Red Hulk. I bet you can guess what color he is. He's purple. Just kidding. Red Hulk is red.

Anger comes from different places and can have many colors. Maybe you are angry because you are sad about something. That could turn you into a blue Hulk. Maybe you are a scared yellow Hulk. You should try to figure out what is making you angry. Knowing what causes your anger will help you better control it.

Anger Busters

Iron Man invented Hulk-buster armor that was powerful enough to battle a rampaging, out-of-control Hulk. You will need your own anger busters to fight your anger. Here are just a few options:
- Draw a picture of your anger and then tear it up.
- Shout into a pillow or give it a strong squeeze.
- Knock over some Lego towers.
- Get active by doing jumping jacks or running outside.
- Make tight fists, like giant Hulk fists. Squeeze them tight and then release them.

Hulk Breathe!

Try focusing on your breathing to calm down. It is a simple trick to learn.

- Sit up straight in a comfortable position.
- Breathe in deep through your nose.
- As you breathe out, open your mouth, stick out your tongue, and make a roar like the Hulk!
- Repeat five times in a row.

Bruce used the motto "Hulk smashes, Banner builds" to stay positive. Since the Hulk destroyed things, Bruce wanted to build new things. Being positive will help calm anger. How can you turn your Hulk rage into something positive? Maybe head out to the garden and tear out weeds. If you play a musical instrument, pick it up and start playing. Drums are great for rage jams. No instruments? Then just let loose dancing. Swing your arms and kick your legs to loud music. Hulk dancing is so much more fun than Hulk smashing.

When Captain America asked Bruce to get angry and turn into the Hulk to help fight off aliens attacking Manhattan, Bruce responded, "That's my secret, Cap. I'm always angry," and then Hulked out. He was not saying he actually was angry all day, every day. That would be exhausting! Bruce meant that he knew anger was normal and he could control it. Always try to control your anger like Bruce did so it does not control you!

103

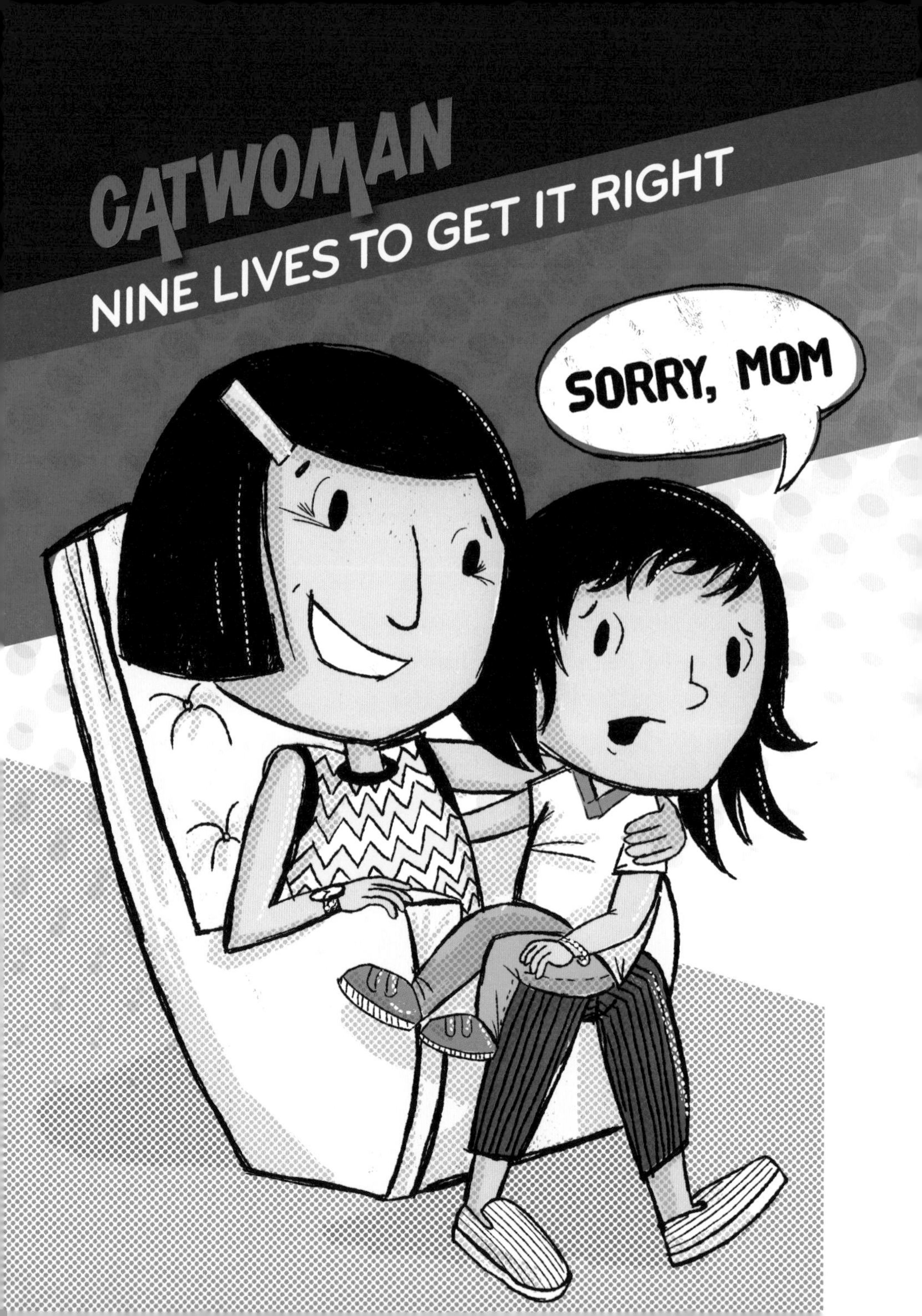
CATWOMAN
NINE LIVES TO GET IT RIGHT
SORRY, MOM

Bats shouldn't have all the fun at night. A talented but troubled woman lurks the alleyways of Gotham City, taking whatever she needs and wants...until she learns she can make a better life for herself.

Selina Kyle always ran from one bad situation to another. After her parents died, Selina lived alone on the streets. She learned to steal in order to survive. She discovered she was quite good at it. From picking pockets to larger robberies, Selina kept getting better as a thief. After she saw Batman for the first time, she decided to wear a costume when she committed crimes. Catwoman was born! Selina was a criminal, but she still had a good heart. She always looked after others who lived in the rough East End neighborhood in Gotham City. She and Batman battled often, but over the years they worked together as Catwoman began to fight crime rather than committing it.

CATWOMAN

For many years, Catwoman was stuck in a loop of bad behavior.

Once you get stuck in a loop of bad behavior, you might start to think you are a bad person. You see other people being good. You think you will never be like them so you might as well keep being bad. Guess what? You do not have to be the bad guy if you do not want to be.

Catwoman breaks out or gets released

Catwoman commits a crime

Catwoman is locked in Arkham Asylum

Batman catches her

The Right Thing, the Wrong Way

You might be tempted to cheat or steal if you think you are doing it for the right reasons. Catwoman would steal often to help out others in her neighborhood, like her friend Holly Robinson. She would also steal from other bad guys so no innocent people were being harmed. You cannot do good by doing bad. Letting a friend copy your homework so they get a better grade is still cheating. Taking something from someone you do not like to give to someone you do like is still stealing.

Earning Back Trust

If you are caught lying or misbehaving, your parents might tell you that they can no longer trust you. It hurts to hear someone no longer trusts you, but you can earn that trust back! Catwoman showed she could be trusted many times by helping Batman fight villains like Hush and Bane. Batman rewarded Catwoman with his most trusted secret. He told her he was actually Bruce Wayne. Catwoman protected that secret, even when others like Poison Ivy tried to get it out of her. Once you break out of your bad behavior loop, you can show others that you deserve their trust.

"I'm sorry for..."

The first step toward changing your behavior is to apologize. Apologizing is more than just saying "I'm sorry." You have to admit what you did wrong.

- Did you take something that was not yours?
- Did you tell a lie?
- Did you cheat on a quiz?

Say what you are sorry for. After you admit what you did, you should explain how you will be better in the future.

Sneaky Cat

It might seem easier to apologize when you don't mean it if you want to stay out of trouble. Don't give in to that feeling. Only apologize when you mean it. You might think you are being sneaky, but you are only cheating yourself.

Even when Catwoman was doing good, she thought she was a villain. One night, Batman told her, "No matter what, I believe that deep down, you're a really good person." It was great for Batman to believe that, but Catwoman needed to believe it for herself. When you do something wrong and apologize, others forgive you. It is much harder to forgive yourself. It does not matter if you did one bad thing or a dozen bad things. Those were mistakes. You are more than your mistakes. You can be a hero when you are ready to be one.

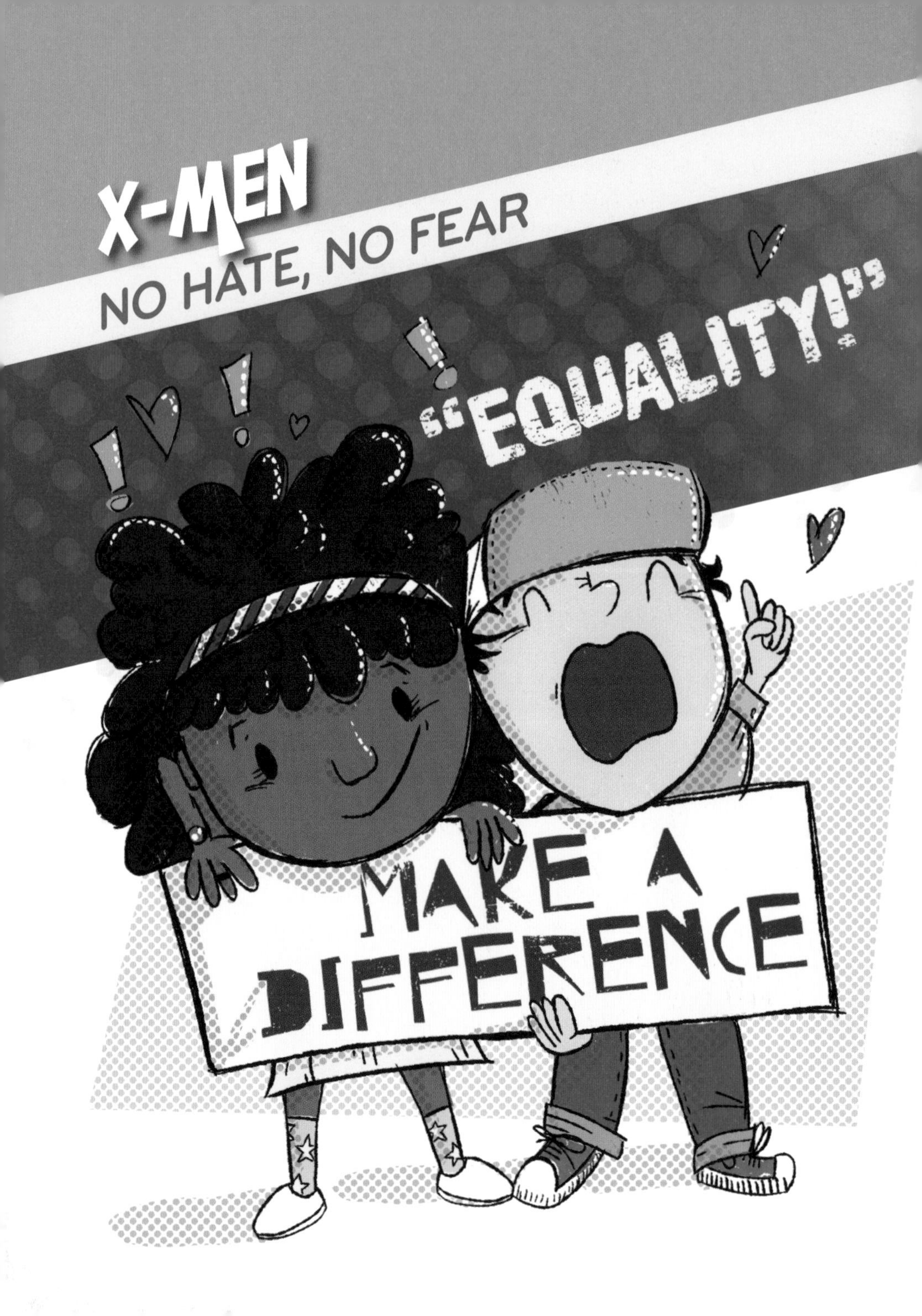

X-MEN
NO HATE, NO FEAR
"EQUALITY!"
MAKE A
DIFFERENCE

In a world that hates and fears them, a group of outsiders with mutant abilities rallies around one man's dream of peace and equality. They study together to control and use their powers...but hope to one day teach the rest of the world there's nothing to fear.

Mutants were feared and hated just because they were born different. As they became teenagers, mutants developed special abilities, and sometimes the way they looked changed. Professor Charles Xavier, a powerful psychic mutant, dreamed that one day humans and mutants could live peacefully together. He opened Xavier's School for Gifted Youngsters as a safe place for mutants, where they could learn how to control their powers. Students at the school could join the X-Men. The X-Men were a superhero team who tried to show the world that mutants did not need to be feared. Many mutants joined and left the X-Men over the years. The team continued to grow and change, but their goal remained the same. They wanted Xavier's dream of peace to come true and were willing to fight for it.

111

X-MEN

The X-Men faced **discrimination** from many people.

Some people in the U.S. government were so afraid of mutants that they wanted to force the mutants into prison camps. That would have violated the mutants' **civil rights**.

Civil rights are basic rights every person has, like freedom of speech, privacy, religion, or a fair trial.

If anyone, including people in the government, wanted to take away civil rights from a person or group of people, the X-Men would be there to stop them. You can, too.

Teamwork

The X-Men split off into many different teams, such as X-Force, X-Factor, and the New Mutants. Each team went on different types of missions. You can start your own team to help fight discrimination in your community by following these steps.

Step 1: Pick a cause. What sort of discrimination do you want to fight?

Step 2: Find your Professor Xavier. You need a parent or teacher to help organize everything.

Step 3: Assemble your team. Ask your friends and classmates to join.

Step 4: Pick roles in the group. Each member of the X-Men has a different power or skill. Your group will be the same way. Maybe one of you is a good writer who can explain your ideas. Another teammate could be a good artist who will make flyers.

Step 5: Select your missions. What goals do you want to set for your team? For example, you could organize a letter-writing campaign to your government officials or raise money with a bake sale.

Discrimination means being treated unfairly because of your skin color, gender, religion, or another difference.

113

X Marks the Safe Space

SAFE!

Professor Xavier's school was a safe space for mutants. Your own school should be a safe space for students targeted with hate and discrimination. Let them know they are protected at school.

- Make signs or flyers that promote support and protection.
- Ask your teachers to hang them on their classroom doors.

Words Used as Weapons

Words can hurt, like when you call someone a mean name because of the color of their skin or their gender. X-Men and other mutants were called "muties." The people who use these mean names are trying to make the other person feel like less of a person. Whether you are part of the group being insulted or just an **ally**, speak out against anyone using those mean words.

An ally is a person who supports others.

No one deserves to feel like less of a person. There is no place for these words in your community.

Being a member of the X-Men means you will fight discrimination. You will also protect anyone who is discriminated against. Confronting bad guys does not mean beating them up. You have to tell them to change their thinking and learn that discrimination is wrong.

ROBIN
A NEW BOY WONDER
IN THE BAT FAMILY

The son of one of the world's greatest heroes and one of the world's worst villains must decide who he wants to be when he grows up...but discovering your place in your family comes with many growing pains.

Damian Wayne was trained by the evil League of Assassins to rule the world one day. When he was ten years old, his mother, Talia, introduced him to his father... Bruce Wayne, the caped crusader Batman! After meeting his father, Damian had a new goal for himself. He wanted to grow up to become an even greater Batman than his father. But first, he had to learn how to fight crime as Batman's partner, Robin! His family grew and changed a lot after he started training with Batman. Robin learned that getting used to his new family was just as challenging as becoming a superhero.

Robin did not have any brothers or sisters, unless you counted the army of Ninja Man-Bats that his mother created.

117

(No one would count an army of Ninja Man-Bats as siblings.) But after Robin went to live with Batman, he met Dick Grayson and Tim Drake, who were Robin before him. They became like siblings.

Siblings do not always get along. Robin beat up Tim the first time they met! And even though he got along a little better with Dick, he still was not always very nice and insulted him a lot. Robin was experiencing **sibling rivalry**.

Your siblings might have something you want, like better toys or being allowed to stay up later. You might think your parents treat your siblings better than you or something else is unfair. These feelings can cause you to fight with your siblings. Fighting with siblings is part of growing up, but a more important part is learning to get along with them.

Don't Tell Me What to Do!

Robin did not just argue with his new siblings. He also argued with his parents. He argued a lot with his mom after he decided he did not want to rule the world like she wanted him to. And he argued with his dad because he thought he had better ways to fight criminals.

Sibling rivalry is when you fight with your brothers or sisters.

Try Being Nice

Robin often told Dick and Tim how much better than them he was. He was unkind by teasing and making fun of them. Treating your siblings this way can quickly turn into a fight. Use kind words instead. If you treat your siblings with kindness, they will do the same. The more Robin teamed up with Dick, the better they got along. Robin eventually decided Dick was his favorite crime-fighting partner. You should play with your siblings instead of fighting with them. You can have more fun together than apart.

It probably felt like his parents were telling him what to do. No one likes being told what to do. It feels like you do not have control over your own life. It is important to remember that your parents care. They are not trying to control you. They just want the best for you.

Family relationships can be tricky. You will not always get along with everyone. When it seems hard, you should remember your family will always support you. Your family is the first and most important team you will ever be on. It will get you ready for future teams like the Justice League and the Teen Titans.

Parent vs. Parent

Sometimes parents argue, too. It is scary to watch or hear. When Batman and Talia fought, the entire world was in danger! It might feel that way for you, too, when your parents argue. It can also make you feel confused or sad. You might think it is your fault they are arguing. All these feelings are normal.

Whatever you are feeling, share it with your parents. It is never your fault. And even if they are not getting along with each other, they still love you.

SQUIRREL GIRL

EATING NUTS AND KICKING BUTTS!

Superheroes just wanna have fun. At least one particular girl with unique squirrel powers does! She saves the day with a smile that can warm even the coldest of supervillain's hearts.

When you grow a big fluffy tail and discover you can talk to squirrels, you might as well become a superhero. That is exactly what Doreen Green decided to do when she became Squirrel Girl. She asked Iron Man if she could be his sidekick, but he said no. But then the evil Doctor Doom captured Iron Man. It was up to Squirrel Girl to save the day. Doctor Doom did not think she was a threat, which was a huge mistake. Squirrel Girl defeated Doctor Doom with her army of squirrels and rescued Iron Man. Even though she beat one of the greatest supervillains alive, she was not always taken seriously. That never stopped Squirrel Girl. She kept being a superhero with a smile on her face. Her positive attitude made her the Unbeatable Squirrel Girl!

123

SQUIRREL GIRL

One of Squirrel Girl's greatest abilities was that she could be incredibly **persuasive**.

Persuasive means being able to convince people to do things.

When Kraven the Hunter came looking to once again try to hunt down Spider-Man, Squirrel Girl talked him out of it.
And when the giant, cosmic Galactus arrived ready to eat Earth, Squirrel Girl persuaded him to eat another planet that was just as nutritious as Earth but without any people on it. Earth was saved, and no one got hurt!

Four Steps to Being Persuasive

1) In a sentence or two, share your opinion in a clear way.
2) Give reasons to support your opinion.
3) Explain your reasons.
4) Restate your opinion with strong, powerful feelings.

SMASH!

These steps are known as the OREO method—Opinion, Reasons, Explanation, Opinion. It is easy to remember and tastier than a planet!

1. Do not eat Earth. Here is another planet.

2. This other planet is filled with healthy nuts and not people.

3. You will no longer be hungry, and Earth will be saved.

4. I really do not want everyone I know to die so please eat this other planet.

THIS ONE!

Positive Attitudes Are Contagious!

When you have a positive attitude, other people will have one, too. Squirrel Girl has that effect on people, even supervillains. After she talked Kraven out of killing Spider-Man, the pair teamed up to defeat the robot villain Ultron. Kraven fighting for the side of good! Can you believe it? Squirrel Girl's positive attitude also worked on the villain Brain Drain. He stopped being bad with Squirrel Girl's help and even enrolled in college with her!

Share your positive attitude with others whenever you can and watch how they change. You could wind up making friends with people you never expected.

Here Are Some Ways to Share a Positive Attitude

- Write someone a friendly note and hide it in a place for them to find.
- Offer to help. A random act of kindness will make anyone's day better.
- Smile. Yes, you can make someone smile just by smiling at them.
- Show off how your squirrel army can cover you like a super suit of armor. (Safety note: Do not attempt with wild squirrels.)

Being a Superhero Is Fun!

Squirrel Girl knows how to keep her superhero life fun and silly. Her motto is "We're here to kick butts and eat nuts." It is impossible to say that motto without giggling. Being a superhero does not mean life has to be a never-ending, gloomy battle. Squirrel Girl proves that a superhero can be as fun as they want. Each adventure brings more happiness. That happiness will make you unstoppable.

HEROIC VIRTUE CHECKLIST

Ally A person who supports others.

Assertiveness Speaking up for yourself and saying what you need.

Confidence Believing in yourself.

Constructive criticism A positive way to tell someone how they can make or do something better.

Creativity Using your imagination to come up with ideas and solve problems.

Determination Trying to do something even if it is difficult.

Encourage To show support to others.

Flexible Being okay with things changing.

Integrity Doing what is right because it is the right thing to do, even if it is hard to do.

Patience Not getting upset if you have to wait for someone or something that takes extra time.

Perseverance Finding a way to overcome any challenge.

Persuasive Being able to convince people to do things.

Questioning Authority Asking whether something is right, even if a parent or teacher is telling you it is.

Resilience Bouncing back quickly from something difficult.

Responsibility Doing something you are supposed to do or acting a way you should act.

Restraint Stopping and thinking before doing something instead of just doing it.

Role model Someone who inspires people to be better and try harder. They set examples that others want to follow.

Self-esteem How you feel about yourself.

Selflessness Being concerned with the needs of others instead of your own wishes.

Taking responsibility Admitting when something is your fault.

Trust Knowing you can count on someone or something.

129

INDEX

INDEX

133

INDEX

U

V

W

X

Y

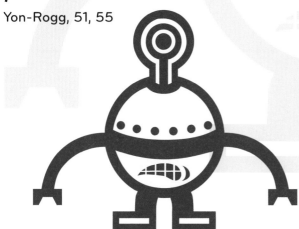

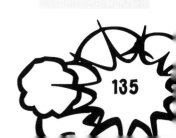

CITATIONS

p. 10 *Superman*, 1978, directed by Richard Donner

p. 12 *All-Star Superman* #10, 2008, written by Grant Morrison and illustrated by Frank Quitely

p. 18 *Black Panther*, 2018, directed by Ryan Coogler

p 25 *Batman* #665, 2007, written by Grant Morrison and illustrated by Andy Kubert

p. 27 *Amazing Fantasy* #15, 1962, written by Stan Lee and illustrated by Steve Ditko

p. 28 *Captain America: Civil War*, 2016, directed by Anthony Russo and Joe Russo

p. 35 *Wonder Woman*, 2017, directed by Patty Jenkins

p. 40 *Captain America: The First Avenger*, 2011, directed by Joe Johnston

p. 55 *Captain Marvel* #1, 2014, written by Kelly Sue DeConnick and illustrated by David Lopez

p. 63 *Annihilation: Conquest* #2, 2008, written by Dan Abnett and Andy Lanning and illustrated by Tom Raney

p. 77 *Ms. Marvel* #2, 2014, written by G. Willow Wilson and illustrated by Adrian Alphona

p. 103 *Indestructible Hulk* #2, 2012, written by Mark Waid and illustrated by Leinil Francis Yu
The Avengers, 2012, directed by Joss Whedon

p. 109 *Catwoman* #1, 2002, written by Ed Brubaker and illustrated by Darwyn Cooke

p. 127 *The Unbeatable Squirrel Girl* #4, 2015, written by Ryan North and illustrated by Erica Henderson

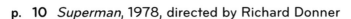